The Drygulch Trail

When Will Curtis rides into Junction City on a cold, rainy night, all he wants is a shot of whiskey and a place to dry off. Instead, he finds himself dragged into a feud between a land-hungry banker and the tough homesteaders who are desperate to keep their ranches. But when rich bully Clem Dawson brings in hired guns to force the ranchers off their land, Curtis decides there is only one thing a decent man could do under the circumstances—and that is to fight. He must keep his wits about him and his pistol handy as he rides The Drygulch Trail.

The Drygulch Trail

Ned Oaks

First published in Great Britain 2016

ISBN 978-0-7198-1893-6

The Crowood Press
The Stable Block
Crowood Lane
Ramsbury
Marlborough
Wiltshire SN8 2HR

www.crowood.com

Robert Hale is an imprint
of The Crowood Press

Typeset by Catherine Williams, Knebworth

Printed and bound in Great Britain by
CPI Antony Rowe, Chippenham and Eastbourne

CHAPTER ONE

It was nearly midnight when the stranger rode into town.

The rain assailed him as he made his way up Main Street. His horse's hoofs made squishing noises in the thick mud. The man wore a slicker against the relentless rain, and water streamed off the brim of his Stetson, which he'd pulled down low over his lean face.

Only one lantern burned in the street, dangling from a pole in front of the saloon. The man pulled reins in front of the saloon's hitching post and looked up and down the street. Apart from the area where he was sitting, the town was completely dark.

He dismounted and wrapped his reins around the post. One other horse was tied there. He climbed the steps wearily and stood under the awning in front of the batwing doors. He peeled off his slicker and shook the water from it, then did the same with his hat. It was the first time he'd been out of the rain all day.

The man pushed through the batwings into the

saloon. It was a surprisingly clean establishment, albeit a small one. There was a bar along the far wall, the length of the room. The tables and the chairs appeared new. There was a large and ornate mirror behind the bar. The brass lanterns had been polished recently. To the man's left, a staircase led up to a landing on the second floor. A pair of closed doors opened onto the landing.

Apart from the stranger, there were two people in the saloon. One was a man sitting on a stool at the far right of the bar, his back turned to the man standing just inside the batwings. The other was a young woman standing behind the bar. She was wiping a glass, her eyes cast down, when the man stepped into the room. The hinges of the batwings creaked and she raised her eyes toward the stranger.

He was a tall man, somewhere around twenty-five years old. He was lean but sinewy. He had light-brown hair and several days' worth of stubble bristled across his jaw. He unbuttoned his sheepskin coat with his right hand and began to walk toward the bar, holding his slicker and hat in his left hand. His coat fell open as he strode forward, revealing a large Navy Colt strapped to his right hip.

When he reached the bar he placed his slicker and hat on one stool and sat down on another.

'Evening, ma'am,' he said amiably. Fatigue was evident in his face. He fingered the makings from his pocket and began to construct a cigarette on the bar.

'Good evening, sir,' the young woman said. 'You look like you've had a hard day.'

He grinned crookedly and poked the cigarette between his lips.

'It's been a long one, that's for sure,' he said, the cigarette bobbing as he spoke. He thumb-snapped a match and held it to his smoke.

'Would you like something to drink while you dry off?'

He nodded. 'Yes, please. Whiskey.'

She brought out a shot glass and filled it with the dark liquid.

'That should warm you up,' she said with a smile.

The man tossed the whiskey back and put his glass back on the bar. She quickly refilled it. He sipped slowly at this one and smiled back at her.

She was a pretty girl, a little over twenty, the man thought. She had lustrous red hair, with a sprinkling of freckles across her nose and under her eyes, which were green.

He extended his hand. 'Name's Will Curtis,' he said.

She shook his hand. 'Sally Bannerman.'

'Pleased to make your acquaintance, Miss Bannerman.'

She released his hand and he went back to sipping his drink.

'You just passing through?' she asked.

'Yes, ma'am,' he said.

'What brings you to this part of Oregon? The

constant rain?' There was a twinkle in her eye and Curtis laughed.

'The rain I could do without,' he said. 'But I don't mind the company.'

She smiled again and was just about to say something else when a fist pounded hard on the counter at the other end of the bar. Sally Bannerman and Will Curtis turned their heads in that direction simultaneously.

'Sally!' the man at the end of the bar bellowed. 'Another drink!' There was no friendliness in his tone. His statement was an order.

Curtis watched Sally walk toward the man, who was meticulously dressed in a pinstriped suit with a massive gold watch chain across his vest. He was a little older than Curtis, with light-blond hair and a small build. When he saw Curtis looking at him, he turned his head and looked back, his lips curled in a sneer.

'What're you looking at, stranger?' the man snarled, his tongue thick from the alcohol he'd consumed.

Curtis shrugged. 'You,' he said simply. His gaze didn't waver.

The man held Curtis's eyes for a few more seconds, then lowered his own to his glass as Sally Bannerman poured whiskey into it.

'Now Alvin, you remember what your father told me,' she said, her voice clear. 'After five drinks I'm to cut you off.'

'Yeah, yeah,' the man said, waving her away.

She hesitated for a moment before walking back

toward Will Curtis.

'He seems fun,' Curtis said drily.

She coaxed a faint smile to her lips.

'Not especially,' she said. She flicked her eyes quickly down the bar and then looked back at Curtis. 'That's Alvin Dawson. His pa owns most of this town.'

Curtis arched an eyebrow. 'That explains his courtesy toward ladies.'

The batwings creaked behind him and he looked at the doorway's reflection in the mirror. A huge man stood there, his eyes rapidly scanning the room. When he espied Alvin Dawson at the corner of the bar he moved toward him.

Curtis watched in the mirror as the man walked across the room. He wore a dark-brown trench coat and large white Stetson. A long black beard descended from his face down to the center of his chest. Curtis discerned a brutality in the man's immobile features. He sat down beside Dawson, who seemed startled to see him for a moment. Then Dawson smiled.

'Evans,' he said, a little nervously. 'What're you doing here?'

Evans cuffed his hat toward the back of his head and sighed, a smile tugging at the corners of his mouth.

'You know why I'm here, Alvin. Your pa sent me.'

Dawson guffawed. 'It's past the old man's bedtime,' he said.

'Well, he ain't asleep,' Evans retorted.

Sally Bannerman carried a glass and the bottle of

whiskey down to where Evans was sitting. She poured him a drink and he downed it in one gulp.

'Another,' he said.

She complied and he dispatched the liquor quickly. He belched loudly and rose.

'I got to piss,' he announced. He stood up and walked around Alvin Dawson. A door in the corner of the room led outside to the alley. Evans opened it and stepped outside, leaving the door ajar behind him.

Dawson looked up at Sally and pushed his glass across the bar toward her.

'More whiskey,' he said.

'Alvin, your pa gave strict orders that I'm to cut you off after five drinks. You know that.'

Will Curtis turned his head to watch the exchange.

'Aw, don't go starting that again,' Dawson moaned. 'Just shut your mouth and do as you're told.'

The woman's face flushed. Curtis continued to watch, saying nothing.

'Alvin, I don't think—' she began, but her words were cut off when Dawson slammed both hands down hard on the bar.

'Goddamn it, you bitch! You just don't know when to leave it alone, do you?'

He reached across the bar and gripped Sally Bannerman's arm, wrenching it painfully. She gasped and dropped the bottle onto the counter. Whiskey spilled out. Dawson grabbed the bottle and turned it upright, still holding tightly to the woman's arm.

'Alvin, stop! You're hurting me,' she said. Outrage suffused her voice.

Alvin Dawson laughed harshly and then shoved her back toward the wall behind her. He lifted the bottle and was about to refill his shot glass when a shadow to his left caused him to turn his head.

Will Curtis pulled the half-empty bottle from Dawson's fingers.

'I don't know who your pa is, smartass,' Curtis said through teeth clenched with anger. 'But it's too bad he never took the time to teach you some manners. Now I guess I've got to do it for him.'

Dawson's mouth was agape as Curtis spoke, as if no one had ever dared to speak to him in such a manner. His nostrils flared with rage.

'How the hell are you going to teach me, you lowdown sheep-herder?' Dawson asked.

'Well, like this, for starters,' Curtis responded.

He raised the bottle and brought it down with all of his strength across Alvin Dawson's brow. The bottle shattered and blood spilled out from the man's hairline, flowing freely down his face. Dawson fell against the bar and then toward Curtis, who kindly stepped aside and allowed him to fall hard onto the plank floor of the saloon.

Curtis raised his eyes to Sally Bannerman's.

'You won't have to worry about him having a sixth drink,' he said. 'He's done for the night.'

He turned and walked back to his stool in front of

the mirror. He resumed sipping slowly at his whiskey.

Sally Bannerman stood perfectly still, watching Curtis with widened eyes.

'Mr Curtis, I think you're going to have to leave,' she said, her voice trembling just slightly. She looked toward the door through which Evans had disappeared. 'Right now.'

Curtis polished off the last of his whiskey and wiped his lips with the back of his hand.

'What's the rush?' he asked.

Sally realized that his nonchalance wasn't an act.

'If Evans comes back and sees this—' she began.

The door burst open all the way and Evans's massive frame filled the doorway.

'What the hell is going on here?' he exclaimed. His eyes fell upon the inert form sprawled on the floor. He stepped into the room and nudged Alvin Dawson with the toe of his boot. There was no response. Blood dripped from the wound on Dawson's forehead onto the floor.

'I think your little friend is having a nap,' Curtis said. 'I guess learning to treat a lady with respect exhausted him.'

Evans raised his head, raking his eyes across Will Curtis.

'What'd you say?' he asked.

Curtis turned sideways to face Evans, resting his left elbow on the bar as he did so.

'So you're deaf as well as ugly?' he asked.

Evans's eyebrows shot up incredulously. He stepped past Dawson and stared hard at the drifter at the other end of the bar.

'You just hit Alvin Dawson,' Evans explained. 'Do you know who his pa is?'

Curtis emitted a threadbare chuckle.

'No, I don't. You his pa's errand boy?'

Evans stiffened. 'Let's just say I handle things for Clem Dawson,' he said. 'He's a big man around these parts. He don't like strangers.' He paused for a moment and looked down again at the man on the floor. 'Especially strangers who beat up his kid.'

'Has Clem Dawson met his kid?' Curtis asked sarcastically. 'He might end up wanting to slap the brat around a little, too.'

Evans moved back the sides of his trenchcoat, revealing a Colt .44 in his holster. Curtis pushed himself away from the bar. He moved a chair out of the way so that the space between himself and Evans was unobstructed. His right hand dangled near his holster.

'What's your name?' Evans asked.

'Will Curtis.'

'You ready to die, Will Curtis?'

Curtis smiled sourly.

'Ready as I'll ever be.'

Evans's eyes narrowed. Curtis expected him to draw at any moment, but the man stayed still. Curtis decided it was fear. Like Alvin Dawson, Evans wasn't a man who was used to being challenged. He seemed confused by the turn of events in this quiet little town where he intimidated almost everyone.

Curtis was tired of waiting.

'Make your move. Otherwise quit wasting my time,' he said, his tone clipped.

Evans waited a moment longer, then his hand blurred toward his gun. By the time he cleared leather, Curtis had already dragged his Navy Colt from its holster and leveled it with the other man's chest. The pistol roared and flame erupted from the muzzle.

Evans stumbled, his gun tumbling from his fingers onto the floor. He looked down at his chest. Blood was spreading from a hole in his sternum. He clawed desperately at his shirt, ripping off a couple of buttons, then his eyes rolled back and he collapsed awkwardly, toppling over a table with a loud crash as he fell.

He was dead before he hit the floor.

CHAPTER TWO

The smell of powdersmoke was thick in the air in the seconds after Evans fell to the floor. Curtis slid his pistol back into its holster and slowly exhaled. He swiveled his head toward Sally Bannerman, whose face was contorted with horror at what she'd just witnessed.

'Sorry, ma'am,' Curtis said sincerely. 'The man was going to draw on me no matter what.'

Her green eyes regarded Curtis for a moment. She seemed to regain her composure.

'Mr Curtis, I thank you for coming to my aid. I'm sorry it led to this,' she said, gesturing toward the two men lying motionless on the floor.

'Some people just want to have a quarrel, come hell or high water,' Curtis asserted.

One of the doors opened upstairs and Curtis turned to see an elderly man descending the steps in his pajamas, a shotgun clutched in his hands. The man looked from Sally to Curtis, and then to the men on the floor.

'What in God's name happened?' he cried.

'Pa, this is Will Curtis,' Sally said, pointing at the drifter. Curtis nodded at the man with the shotgun. 'Alvin Dawson got rough with me and Mr Curtis stepped in. That's when Evans came in and started the gunfight.'

'He lost,' Curtis said, deadpan.

'You better hit the trail, and quick,' the old man said to Curtis. 'Someone's bound to have heard that gunshot. We'll have visitors soon.' The man came the rest of the way down the staircase and extended a hand toward Will Curtis. 'I thank you for coming to my daughter's aid. Not a lot of men around here who would stick their necks out like that. My name's Cecil Bannerman.'

Curtis took the man's hand and shook it.

'Pleased to meet you, sir.'

The old man looked down at Evans's corpse.

'Tabor Evans,' he said. 'I always figured he'd end up this way. No-good sidewinder for as long as I've known him.' He glanced at his daughter. 'You doing OK, honey?'

She nodded. 'I'm fine, Pa. Probably just have a bruise on my arm where he squeezed me.'

Sally Bannerman had barely finished her sentence when the batwings parted and a baldheaded man looked through. He took in the situation at a glance and backed out of the doorway into the night again.

'Earl Jackson,' muttered Cecil Bannerman. 'Damnit. It won't be long before more of Dawson's boys show up.' He gestured toward his daughter. 'Sally, you get ready right quick and take Mr Curtis out to your uncle's place.'

Without a word, Sally came out from behind the counter and ran up the steps. Curtis heard a door open upstairs. Bannerman faced him.

'My brother died a couple months ago,' he explained. 'Left us his property. There's a cabin there where you can hole up.'

'My horse wouldn't make it far right now anyway,' Curtis noted. 'I'll be happy to borrow your cabin for a brief spell.'

'Good,' Bannerman said. He sighed heavily. 'I'm afraid you rode into town at a bad time, Mr Curtis. Lot of bad stuff happening around here these days.' He pointed at Alvin Dawson. 'Mostly because of him and his pa.'

'His pa's got a lot of money, huh?'

'Yes, he does. But he wants more. Lots more. And he figures the people of this town are either going to help him get richer or pay for his failure.'

Curtis frowned. 'What's his game?' he asked.

'He owns the bank and almost half of the businesses in town,' Bannerman said. His face was somber. 'Now he aims to go into the ranching business. He's been putting the squeeze on a lot of the local homesteaders, including my brother.'

Just then they heard the door close upstairs and watched Sally Bannerman race down the steps. She wore a flannel shirt, Levis, and a dark floppy hat, along with riding-boots.

'Ready?' she asked Curtis coolly.

'Hell, yes,' he responded. He shook hands with Cecil Bannerman again. 'Thank you, sir.'

'No, thank *you*,' Bannerman replied. 'Something like this was bound to happen, with the men Clem Dawson's been bringing to town. You just happened to be the match that lit the fuse, so to speak.' He shook his head quickly. 'All right, enough jawing—you two head out. Sally, after you get Mr Curtis settled, head on out to your brother's place. I'll come over tomorrow afternoon.'

She nodded and led Curtis through the batwings. He donned his slicker and hat again, then unhitched his horse from the post.

'This way,' she said, leading him to an alley between the saloon and the livery next door. He cast a quick glance down Main Street and observed lights in a large house several doors down from the Bannermans' establishment.

'That Clem Dawson's house?' Curtis asked.

She looked where he pointed .

'Yep,' she said. They both saw human shapes stirring in the shadows in the front yard of the Dawson place. 'We got to get going.'

She walked rapidly down the pitch-dark alleyway. It was barely wide enough for Curtis's horse, which he led by the reins, following closely behind the young woman. They emerged into a much wider alley that ran along behind the buildings on Main Street. She led them across the alley to a small stable where she and her father kept both of their horses. A little over two minutes later she had saddled her horse and was ready to ride.

They both mounted after she led her horse from the stable and closed the door behind them. Loud voices were coming from the front of the saloon.

'Looks like Pa has company,' Sally said. She neck-reined her horse around and touched spurs to its flanks. The animal took off quickly, cantering back in the direction from which Will Curtis had come to town. He spurred his animal to follow her and they rode into the darkness, the only light coming from the silvery moon that loomed above the forested peaks around the town.

It was about an hour before they reached the cabin.

Sally Bannerman led Will Curtis out of town and through the foothills, taking a circuitous route that avoided the main road. They emerged from the trees and pulled leather on the edge of a misty forest pasture. The cabin was a dozen yards from the rim of the trees. It was completely dark, with shuttered windows.

'This is it,' she said. 'There's a little barn around back where you can put your horse.'

They dismounted and led their horses by the reins to the barn. She tied her mount to a pole outside while Curtis led his into a stall. He unsaddled his horse and rubbed it down with a handful of hay. He removed a bag of oats from a saddlebag.

'I'll go in and build a fire while you do that,' Sally said.

'I'll be just a minute,' he said.

She left and before he had finished with his horse he could smell wood smoke coming from the stone chimney at the back of the cabin. He closed the stall and then shut the door to the barn. She had lighted an oil lamp in the kitchen and he could see her through the window as he approached the back door, carrying his bedroll with him.

He opened the door and stepped into the cabin. It was very clean, although a little musty. He closed the door behind him and grinned faintly.

'This is a pretty nice place,' he said.

She was looking in a cupboard near the woodstove and turned around when Curtis spoke. She pushed a stray lock of hair from her face.

'Thanks,' she said. 'My uncle was a very tidy bachelor. I come out every few weeks and air it out, get rid of the dust and cobwebs.'

'I'm sure he'd appreciate that.'

She turned back to the cupboard and removed a tin of coffee. There were also a few cans of beans and a can of strawberries.

'Well, there're a few things here you can eat. And there's plenty of coffee. I'm sure Pa will bring some food out for you when he comes tomorrow.'

Curtis sat down on one of the two chairs by the kitchen table. He removed his hat and laid it over his knee. His eyes were red and weary as he scrubbed a hand down his face.

'You know,' he said with a grin, 'I don't even know the name of your town. I didn't see any signs when I rode in.'

'It's Junction City,' she said. 'Where are you from originally?'

'Hard to say,' he said. 'I've lived in lots of places around the Oregon and Idaho line.'

'What brings you around here?'

'Oh, just drifting around mostly. Never been to the Willamette Valley and always heard about it, so I thought I'd check it out myself.' He wiped some dirt from his palm onto the leg of his pants. 'My sister and her husband own a place down by the California border. I figured if I didn't find anything to do around here then I'd mosey on down there a spell.'

'What do you think so far?' she asked with a sardonic smile.

'It ain't boring, that's for sure.'

'Not right now, anyway,' she said. 'It was different before Clem Dawson came to town.'

'How long ago was that?'

She considered the question. 'Probably around five years ago, now.'

Curtis took out the makings and began to roll a smoke.

'Where'd he come from?'

'Portland, I think,' she said. 'I got the impression he wanted to be a big fish in a little pond, if you know what I mean.'

'I do,' Curtis said. 'Looks like he succeeded.'

Her mouth tightened. 'Not in an honest or decent way, he didn't. He did it by bullying people and hiring thugs to get what he wanted.'

Curtis licked the cigarette paper and scraped a match down the heel of his boot. Cigarette smoke billowed out of his mouth as he listened to Sally speak.

'Alvin's just as bad as his pa, but in a different way,' she continued. 'He's always pawing after girls, whether they like him or not.'

Curtis blew a smoke ring and poked his finger through it.

'Who in hell'd like that little yellow belly?' he asked.

'Good question.'

He chuckled and took another drag.

'How did Evans fit into all this?' he asked. 'Or is he paid to be Little Alvin's nanny?'

'He is – er, *was* Clem Dawson's enforcer. Part of his job was keeping Alvin under control.'

'He a drunk?'

'Not always, but he has his moments. Especially when he and his pa are fighting. That's when Evans stepped in to keep Alvin in line.' She arched an eyebrow. 'As you saw tonight, it didn't always work.'

Curtis grunted inscrutably, pondering the situation into which he'd wandered.

'What about the law?' he asked finally. 'Ain't there a sheriff around here, or a town marshal?'

'There are deputy sheriffs in Eugene,' she said. 'But

they don't come out to Junction City very often. Plus, Clem Dawson has deep pockets. He's become a good friend to the sheriff. It's an open secret around here – the bribery, that is.'

'Well, what are the locals around here going to do about it?' There was a tinge of exasperation in Curtis's voice.

'I don't know,' she said tentatively. Her face darkened slightly. 'Now that Dawson's planning on becoming a big landowner, the people out here in the hills are starting to feel the pinch, too. Used to be he limited his harassment to the city folk, like my pa. The farmers and ranchers turned a blind eye most of the time. Now they can't afford to do that, unless they're willing to let Dawson ride roughshod over them.'

'How many of them stand up to him?'

She shook her head sadly. 'Not many. My uncle did, when Dawson came out here and made him a cash offer. Uncle Chuck told him to go to hell. Not long after that they tried to burn down the cabin with him in it.'

'I'll be damned,' Curtis said quietly.

'Luckily he was a light sleeper. He came out with his rifle and scared Dawson's men away before the fire spread. He was able to put it out himself.'

'So Dawson's willing to murder innocent people to get what he wants?' Curtis asked in a grim voice.

'Oh, he won't hesitate to murder someone if that's what he thinks needs to be done.'

'What are you and your pa going to do?'

Her even white teeth tugged pensively at her bottom lip.

'I don't know,' she said. 'Especially after tonight. I think we might just have to sell up and leave town.'

'I'm sorry I made it worse for y'all.'

She met his gaze. 'There was going to be a confrontation with Clem Dawson or his son one way or another, Mr Curtis. Please don't apologize. I'm just relieved that you weren't hurt or killed.'

Curtis's face brightened. 'Mighty kind of you, ma'am,' he said. He stifled a yawn and looked down the hallway. 'Well, I better be getting some shut-eye. I got to be ready for anything come morning.'

'Yes, of course,' she said, slightly embarrassed. She stepped toward the back door. 'Please just make yourself at home. You might want to keep the windows shuttered and only build a fire at nighttime. Dawson's men might come snooping around here.' She turned the handle on the door. 'My pa will be here in the afternoon to check in with you. Take care, Mr Curtis.'

Curtis rose and smoothed down his greasy hair.

'Thank you, Miss Bannerman. I hope to see you again, real soon.'

She smiled shyly and stepped out, closing the door behind her. Within twenty minutes Curtis was asleep in his blankets on a cot in one of the bedrooms. His rifle was leaning against the wall beside the bed, and on a table nearby was his Navy Colt.

*

Cecil Bannerman came early the next afternoon. His face wore an anxious expression. Will Curtis came out from the back door to meet him.

'Morning, Mr Bannerman.'

'Call me Cecil,' the old man said, dismounting a few feet from Curtis. 'As long as I can call you Will.'

'I wouldn't have it any other way,' Curtis said. He noticed Bannerman was wearing a pistol on his belt. 'Everything all right in Junction City?'

'For the time being. A couple of Dawson's men showed up right after y'all left last night. They took Alvin home, and then Clem Dawson himself made an appearance. I told them a stranger had come and killed Evans and knocked out Alvin, and that I didn't know anything more than that.'

'Did they ask where Sally went?'

'Yeah, they did. I said she was so upset by the gunplay that she'd ridden out to her brother's place. I told them you lit out right after shooting Evans and that I thought you were headed for the California border.'

'Has Alvin woke up yet?'

Bannerman smiled. 'Just this morning. Evidently he doesn't remember anything about last night.' He tied his horse to a pole outside the barn and removed a burlap sack containing biscuits, jerky, and bacon from one of his saddlebags. 'I brought this for you. Should keep your belly full for a couple of days. I don't think it'll be safe to ride out before then. Dawson's got some of his men combing the hills looking for you. They won't check here, though. It's too far out of the way.'

He hefted the sack and handed it over to Curtis.

'Thanks, Cecil. I appreciate it.'

'Not a problem. And by the way, I was thinking about something ...' Bannerman said a little tentatively.

'What's that?' Curtis asked.

'Well, I figure you've probably done quite a bit of ranch work.' Curtis nodded. 'My son has a hundred-acre spread a little east of here. I know he's been needing some help, but he has a hard time finding it because Dawson's men tend to run off strangers – especially strangers who are good with a gun and know how to run a ranch.' Bannerman paused and cleared this throat. 'Anyway, what I'm getting at is maybe you'd like to stick around a while and do some work for my boy. What d'ya think?'

Curtis pursed his lips thoughtfully. 'I don't want to bring Dawson's men down on your son.'

'Don't you worry about that,' Bannerman said confidently. 'Abe can handle himself.' He held up a hand. 'Just let me talk it over with him today. I have to go out there and get Sally. I'll come back by in a few hours and let you know. You can think it over in the meantime.'

'All right,' Curtis said. 'I got no problem with that.'

'Good. Now you get yourself something to eat.'

Bannerman untied his horse and clambered up into the saddle. Curtis watched him ride out across the yard and disappear into the trees. He went back into the cabin and made himself a meal while he waited for Bannerman to return.

Hours passed. Curtis was sleepy after his meal and took a nap on the cot in the bedroom. He was surprised to awake and find that Bannerman still hadn't returned. He lay in the cot for a few minutes, dozing lazily, then decided to make some coffee. He was boiling water in the kitchen when some movement in the trees across the yard caught his attention through the grimy kitchen window.

It was a horse. More importantly, Curtis realized after a moment, it was Cecil Bannerman's horse. There was no sign of the saloon owner, although the animal still had a saddle cinched around its middle.

The hair was already bristling on the back of Curtis's neck when the horse halted near the back door. Curtis opened the door to take a closer look. He saw thick smears of wet blood on the empty saddle, leading in a stream down a strap to the right stirrup. Drops of blood fell from the edge of the stirrup onto the grass.

'Judas priest!' Curtis whispered to himself.

His hand flashed to his hip and palmed the Colt in one smooth movement. He backed into the kitchen and kicked the back door closed. He stepped toward the kitchen window and moved into the shadows by the wall. He had a good view of the south side of yard then, and he was in a position where no one outside could get a good view of him.

His eyes scanned the trees across the yard, where

Bannerman's horse had emerged. It wasn't long before he saw movement among the branches. He sucked in a sharp breath when he saw two horsemen ride into the yard and walk their horses toward the back of the cabin.

They moved out of Curtis's line of sight and he took the opportunity to cat-foot down the hallway into the living room. He was glad that all of the windows were shuttered except for the two in the kitchen. Once in the living room, he stood in a position in which he could see down the hallway without being observed by the men in the yard.

There was a window in the back door and through it Curtis observed the two horsemen pull reins by the woodpile. He could see them more clearly now, and he recognized their breed instantly. They were hardcases, hired guns. Curtis had no doubt whom they worked for and why they were here. They were Dawson's men, and they must have been following Cecil Bannerman.

Judging from the amount of blood on Bannerman's saddle, the old man was either dead or dying. No one could lose that much blood and still be on his feet.

He watched the men tie their mounts to the pole outside the barn. One of them took the reins of Bannerman's horse and looked it over, saying something as he did so that made the other man chortle. Curtis couldn't hear what they were saying, just the mumbling of voices.

Adrenaline flowed through Curtis when he saw them approach the back door. The first man leaned toward the window in the door. He shaded his eyes with his hand and looked into the kitchen. Then he reached down and opened the door.

Curtis, lurking in the shadows of the living room, knew what was coming. If these men found him, and he assumed they soon would, then they would try to kill him. He had been around and seen enough professional killers to know these men's methods. He would have to kill them if he wanted to get out of this cabin alive. Curtis thumbed back the hammer and waited, unconsciously holding his breath.

The door pushed open and the men stepped cautiously into the kitchen. Curtis backed further out of sight. His pulse pounded in his ears and everything seemed to be moving slowly.

'Anyone here?' one of the men called. 'We're looking for Cecil Bannerman. He around?'

Curtis was silent, his body tensed for whatever was about to take place.

The men were in the first bedroom now. He heard them move a few things around and then step back into the hallway. They were moving toward the second bedroom, where his bedroll and rifle were. They would know someone was in or around the cabin when they saw Curtis's things. He decided to act while there was still an element of surprise in his favor.

He swiveled away from the wall toward the hallway and raised his pistol.

'Afternoon, gentlemen,' he said evenly. 'Out for a little bushwhacking?'

The men froze in place, staring at Curtis in shock. Neither had a pistol in hand. Curtis suspected they hadn't tangled with anyone around Junction City who gave them a run for their money. That was why they'd gotten sloppy.

'Who the hell are you?' the first man asked with a sneer.

'This is private property,' Curtis said. 'Trespassing is against the law, you know.'

'We ain't stealing nothing,' the second man said. 'Like we said, we're just looking for Cecil Bannerman.'

'Shut up,' Curtis commanded. 'You're lying. Now pull out your pistols and throw them on the floor, nice and slow.'

The men exchanged glances before moving to obey Curtis's order. The first man pulled out his pistol and lobbed it a few feet ahead of him onto the wooden floor.

'Now you,' Curtis said to the second man.

'You got it,' the man responded.

He was dragging the pistol out of its holster when he made his move. His partner crouched and leapt forward onto the floor while the big man behind him drew. The man was confident of his abilities, probably mistaking Curtis for a local cowpunch without much skill in the gun department.

Curtis was momentarily distracted by the man on the floor, and the second gunslinger was able to get a shot off. It hit the wall inches away from Curtis's face, shearing off shards of wood. Curtis fired without aiming and made a lucky shot. The bullet went straight into the second man's throat, causing a grotesque spray of blood to spurt across the wall in the hallway. The man dropped his gun into the bedroom doorway and grabbed for his throat, trying to stop the bleeding with his hands. Blood oozed between his fingers, flowing freely from the severed artery in his neck. He fell forward onto his knees, held steady there for a moment, then collapsed onto his partner's legs just as the latter reached desperately for his own pistol. Pinned by the dead weight of his partner's corpse, the drygulcher screamed in helpless terror, his outstretched fingers falling short of touching the gun by mere centimeters.

'Golly, you really want that gun, don't you?' Curtis asked. He stepped forward and brought the heel of his boot down on the man's fingers.

'No!' the killer said. 'Oh, please!'

Curtis crushed the man's fingers under his boot, feeling the snap of bone and cartilage. He lifted his other foot and put all of his body weight on the man's hand. The man released a wail of pain such as Curtis had never heard in his life.

'Where's Bannerman?' Curtis asked coldly, releasing a bit of the pressure from beneath his boot.

'Let me go, please! Oh, God – my fingers!' the man bleated.

Curtis leaned down a little closer.

'I guess you didn't hear me,' he said. He pressed down with his boot and felt something crunch in one of the fingers beneath it. The man howled, tears streaming down his face.

'I don't know where Bannerman is,' he cried. 'I swear! Just let me go – I'll give you anything!'

'I got all I need,' Curtis said casually. 'And you're a liar. I won't ask you again, feller. Where's Bannerman?'

'He's out there in the woods.'

'Alive?'

'I think so.'

'You shoot him?'

'No,' the man said, jerking his chin toward his partner, whose lifeless body still clung to his ankles. 'He shot him. Got him somewhere below the ribs. I can show you where Bannerman is. You get him to a sawbones in Junction City in a hurry and I bet he pulls through.'

'That's awful Christian of you, friend,' said Curtis witheringly. 'You must have a lot of love for your fellow man.'

He leaned down and picked up the man's gun from the floor, then stepped back, his pistol still fixed on the pinned man, who now held his mangled fingers to his chest, moaning quietly.

'Get up,' Curtis said.

The man pulled himself forward on his elbows, thrashing his legs out from under the corpse. He used his uninjured hand to push himself up and stand before Curtis. A thick film of sweat was layered across the man's face and neck.

'You're going to show me where to find Bannerman,'

said Curtis.

'Then you'll let me go?' the wounded killer whined.

'Hell, no. You'll be lucky if I don't plant a bullet in your brain, you slick little weasel. I'd turn you over to the law, but I've been told what little law there is around here is owned lock, stock and barrel by Clem Dawson. So maybe I'll turn you over to Bannerman's son. I heard he lives not far from here.'

'Honest, sir – I wasn't going to hurt Bannerman. I was just doing what I was paid to do.'

'Which is?'

'Dawson wanted Bannerman followed.'

'Why?'

'Because ... he thought Bannerman might lead us to whoever it was that killed Evans and smashed that bottle over Alvin's face.' The man looked down at Curtis's gun. 'I guess it was you, wasn't it?' Curtis said nothing, and the nervous man continued speaking, trying to calm his own nerves. 'We looked for Bannerman earlier in the afternoon but didn't find him until about a half-hour ago, heading this way.'

Curtis wondered where Sally was.

'Was Bannerman alone?' he inquired sharply.

'Yeah, he was.' The man's mind was racing, searching for any kind of angle that would get him out of the situation. 'I'll show you where to find the old man. I've tried to help you. I've just been doing my job when it came to Bannerman. I didn't know anyone was going to end up dead.'

'Sure you didn't,' said Curtis, not altogether reassuringly. A thought occurred to him. 'Any more of Dawson's boys running around besides you and your late friend?'

A second passed, then the man said, 'No, just us.'

Curtis didn't believe him. He swung the barrel of the gun toward the back door.

'Git,' he said.

The man stepped over his partner and walked toward the kitchen. Curtis followed close behind, the muzzle of his pistol pressed firmly into the man's back. Curtis's shoulder brushed some of the dead man's blood-spatter on the wall as he stepped over the body.

'What's your name?' Curtis asked.

'Kantor,' the other man said, once more holding his injured hand gingerly against his chest. His teeth gritted with pain. 'Mack Kantor.'

'Open the door, Kantor.'

The man did as he was told and seconds later they were standing in the grass behind the house.

'Stop right there,' Curtis said.

He had decided to tie Kantor up before they went to search for Bannerman. He was stepping toward the barn to fetch a rope when the gunshot sounded from the trees. He felt the burn of the slug as it passed his left shoulder, digging a groove through his flannel shirt before passing into the barn wall a few feet away. Curtis swore as pain shot down from his shoulder through the length of his arm.

He pivoted and saw a burst of flame from among the

trees. Another bullet came toward him, thudding into the grass near his feet. He dived behind a stone trough by the barn door. A third bullet ricocheted off the trough and lodged into the barn.

'Kill him!' screamed Mack Kantor. 'Kill that son of a bitch!'

Kantor turned and ran toward the trees, although not in the direction from which the gunfire was coming. Curtis swiped his pistol from the holster and observed Kantor's legs through the gap beneath the trough. He carefully took aim and fired, a wry smile creasing his face.

The bullet hit Kantor in the back of his right ankle, tearing through his Achilles tendon before lodging somewhere in his foot. Kantor leapt into the air, yelling frantically. He hit the ground clutching his ankle with his one good hand and rolled in the grass, howling in pain.

That's for Cecil Bannerman, Curtis thought. Then his grazed shoulder throbbed and his brief moment of satisfaction ended.

CHAPTER THREE

The gunmen had been distracted by Kantor's flailing in the grass, but not for long. Bullets started to pepper the trough and the barn wall above it. From the angle where the gunmen were positioned they were unable to hit Curtis under the trough. The firing went on for a few more minutes, during which Curtis saw Kantor drag himself into the trees on his elbows. Between the crushed hand and the shattered ankle, Kantor probably wouldn't be doing much bushwhacking for a while. Curtis was pleased.

Curtis's ear was near the ground, so he heard the other riders approaching. They were coming from the east, and there were many of them; at least five, he figured. In less than a minute the men in the trees became aware of them, too. The firing ceased and Curtis heard confused voices chattering. Shortly thereafter the men who had been shooting at him were mounted and riding away. Curtis could see some of their movements through the trees. They were heading west, toward Junction City.

Curtis rose cautiously, his eyes peering over the rim of the trough into the maples and firs where the gunmen had been hiding. There was no sign of them, or of Mack Kantor. Curtis assumed that Kantor's friends had helped him mount his horse and leave with them. The appearance of Dawson's other men confirmed Curtis's earlier suspicion about Kantor's veracity when the man had claimed there were no other men in the hills looking for Cecil Bannerman. Lying, however, was probably the least of Mack Kantor's crimes.

The horses were close now. Curtis rose and took a step toward the back of the cabin. The riders burst out of the trees to his left before he could take another step. His hand moved toward his hip but the leader of the riders already his pistol in hand and pointed at Curtis.

'Stop it right there, feller,' the man yelled, pulling on his horse's reins. The other riders followed suit and stopped close behind the leader. 'Put those hands up.'

Curtis cursed silently and obeyed the order.

'What's your name?' the rider asked.

A woman's voice responded before Curtis did.

'Will Curtis,' it said. Then Sally Bannerman rode around to the front of the pack of riders. 'It's all right, Abe. This is the man I told you about.'

The leader of the riders stared hard at Curtis, suspicious of any new faces in the Junction City area, particularly those of strong young men such as Curtis.

Newcomers who fit that description tended to work for Clem Dawson.

'Howdy,' Abe Bannerman said. His expression softened but only a little. Curtis could see a resemblance between Abe and his sister, now that he looked at the man more closely.

'Is my pa here, Mr Curtis?' Sally asked anxiously.

Curtis had a sinking feeling as he shook his head.

'No, ma'am, I'm sorry to say he ain't. His horse rode in alone a while back.' He looked around but didn't see Bannerman's mount. It must have wandered off into the trees. 'I was going to put it in the barn, but then some of Dawson's hired guns showed up.'

Abe Bannerman's mouth fell open. 'You know who it was?' he asked.

'One of them was named Mack Kantor,' said Curtis, who noticed the change on the rider's facial expression at the mention of the name. 'He had a partner with him.'

'Probably Butch Muller,' Sally said, looking toward her brother. He nodded.

'Well, he's still here,' Curtis explained. He pointed toward the cabin. 'He's in there, in the hallway.'

'Tied up?' Bannerman asked.

'Dead,' Curtis said plainly.

Abe Bannerman dismounted, handed his reins to his sister and stepped into the cabin through the back door. Presently he came back out.

'It's Butch Muller all right,' he said.

'They came here asking about your pa,' Curtis said. 'But they knew his horse was running around. They saw it in the yard.' He frowned. 'Did Cecil make it out to your place today, Abe?'

Bannerman shook his head.

'We were expecting him but he never came. That's why we rode out here to look for him.'

Sally was visibly fearful.

'Abe,' she said, 'we need to find Pa. Now.'

'I know it,' he said deliberately. He introduced the three other riders to Curtis. 'Mr Curtis—'

'Call me Will.'

'All right, Will – this is John Wilson, Phil Shirreffs, and Jake Douglas. They're neighbors of mine. They've been having problems with Clem Dawson, too.'

'Pleased to meet you, gentlemen,' said Curtis with a nod.

'Will, would you mind staying here with Sally while we search the woods for my pa?'

'Now, just a minute,' Sally replied, her face flushed with anger. 'That's my pa, too. I don't need to be left behind here like a kid.'

'Sally, there are men still hiding out in the woods. Dawson's men. If we took you along and something happened to you, you know Pa would never forgive me.'

Sally Bannerman was quiet, then nodded reluctantly.

'Fine,' she said. She glanced at Curtis. 'You don't mind staying here?'

'Not at all.' Curtis pointed to the trees on the west

side of the barn. 'That's the direction your pa's horse came from.'

Abe Bannerman put a foot in a stirrup and swung up into the saddle. He pulled the reins and turned the horse around to face where Curtis had pointed.

'All right, fellers,' he said to the other horsemen. 'Let's take a look around.'

The group touched spurs and rode across the yard into the trees.

'I need to reload,' Curtis said, pulling his pistol from the holster. 'I got my rifle in there, too.'

Sally dismounted and led her horse into the barn while Curtis went back into the cabin. When she came out a short time later she saw Curtis dragging Butch Muller's body out of the house. He laid it in the grass behind the barn and covered it with a tarp he found in a lean-to near the woodpile.

Sally got water from the pump and cleaned up the blood in the hallway while they waited for the riders to return. Then she made coffee and sat down at the table, watching Curtis as he looked periodically out the windows for any sign of approaching horsemen.

More than an hour passed before Abe Bannerman returned with the other riders. His blunt features were drawn and grim, telling both Curtis and Sally everything they needed to know.

Sally ran from the back doorway to her brother, who stepped down from his horse and put his arms around her.

'Tell me it's not true, Abe,' she said desperately, tears streaming down her face.

The muscles in Bannerman's jaw clenched, as if to keep him from telling her what he'd found.

'I'm sorry, Sally.' He put his hand over his eyes for a moment and took a deep breath. Having regained his composure, he held his sister against his chest.

Curtis stood by in silence, observing the scene. Anger was rising steadily within him as he thought of Cecil Bannerman, a man whom he had barely known. The brevity of their relationship didn't matter to Curtis. He had liked Bannerman and seen him as a man of integrity. Now that man was dead, killed by Clem Dawson. Beneath the anger and sadness, Curtis also recognized that it had been his own actions in the bar in Junction City that had brought the conflict out into the open. He felt a responsibility to stick around and help Abe and Sally Bannerman – and hurt Clem Dawson.

Sally Bannerman's voice cut through Curtis's somber reverie.

'Where is he, Abe?' she asked. She looked toward the other horsemen. 'What happened to him?'

'He's about a mile from here,' her brother responded carefully. 'I want you to go with Phil and head back to my place for the night.'

'No!' she hollered. 'I want to see him. What if he's not dead, Abe? I can help him, maybe—'

'You can't do anything for him, Sally. I wish you could, but it's too late. And I don't want you to see him like that. Please, just do as I ask.'

'He was my pa, too,' she said, tears streaming anew.

'I know, Sally,' Abe Bannerman said soothingly.

Phil Shirreffs cleared his throat.

'Miss Sally, your brother's just looking out for your feelings,' he said. 'We all respected your pa. I don't think he'd want you to see him like that.'

Her eyes darted to Shirreffs.

'It's that bad, is it?' She looked at her brother. 'It's that bad?'

He nodded slowly and then removed a handkerchief from the inside pocket of his coat. He handed it to her and she wiped her face.

'All right, Phil,' she said finally. 'Let's go back to Abe's.'

'Yes, ma'am,' Shirreffs said.

She brought her mare out of the barn and mounted.

'Thank you, Will,' she said to Curtis, using his first name now. 'We'll all understand if you want to leave after everything that's happened.'

Curtis made a dismissive gesture.

'Miss Bannerman, I'll stick around as long as y'all will have me. It's personal to me now. Your pa wouldn't be dead right now if I hadn't come into your saloon last night. And a man who was paid by Clem Dawson pulled a gun on me last night. He would've killed me if he'd been a little faster. That don't exactly make me take kindly to Dawson.'

Curtis thought there was a new element of respect in

the way Abe Bannerman looked at him.

'We're much obliged to you, Will. If my pa thought highly of you, then that's all I need to know. We'll be glad to have the help. We're going to need it.'

Phil Shirreffs led Sally Bannerman across the yard to where the trail vanished in among the trees. The remaining men watched them depart.

'I'll get my horse,' Curtis said. He returned shortly and mounted.

Abe Bannerman led the way, followed closely by Curtis, Wilson, and Douglas. They found Cecil Bannerman's horse not far away, idly munching grass. Douglas tied a rope to it and brought it with them. It was late afternoon when they emerged from the trees into a small forest clearing and pulled leather. As they did so Curtis observed Cecil Bannerman's body near the edge of the clearing, lying beside the base of a massive maple.

The old man's death had been far more painful and gruesome than Curtis had expected.

He was bound with barbed wire, the spikes cutting into his parchment-like flesh. His throat had been slashed so deeply that his head lolled at an awkward angle. Curtis counted three bullet wounds in his chest.

'My God,' he murmured. 'Who the hell would do something like this?'

'Dawson,' Abe Bannerman said.

'Or the men Dawson pays,' said Jake Douglas. He was a big man with enormously broad shoulders. His clean-shaven features glowed in the late-afternoon sunlight.

'Those hired guns he brought to town will do anything for the right price.'

Curtis nodded. 'I can see that.'

The body was covered in blood, the throat having been cut so deeply that the result had almost been decapitation. This wasn't a typical level of range violence, such as Curtis had encountered at various times in his wanderings. Usually that entailed no more than a bullet to the head or the heart. This was different. Any person who would order a murder like this was interested in more than taking over other people's land – that person wanted to instill terror in anyone who considered resisting him, and was more than willing to employ even the most brutal methods to attain what he desired.

The men dismounted and removed the barbed wire from Bannerman's body. Then they wrapped him in a blanket from John Wilson's saddlebag and secured the blanket with a rope. Curtis helped Douglas secure the body over the late man's horse.

'We'll bury him back at my uncle's place,' Abe Bannerman said.

Dusk had fallen by the time the men completed their task and departed for Abe Bannerman's ranch.

Sally was waiting for them on the porch when they rode in. Wilson, Douglas, and Shirreffs left for their respective homes not long after.

Curtis went into the house and looked around. It

smelled like cooking. Abe Bannerman's wife came out from the kitchen to greet the men. She was a tall, handsome woman with a friendly disposition, although Curtis also detected signs of strain in her prematurely lined face. He wondered how long Clem Dawson had been making things hard for the local homesteaders.

'Pleased to meet you, Will,' Maggie Bannerman said. 'I hope you're hungry.'

Curtis grinned. 'I've never had much trouble rustling up an appetite.'

'Good,' she said. She gestured toward her husband. 'Abe don't eat nearly as much as he used to, ever since these problems with Clem Dawson started.' She searched Bannerman's face. 'God, Abe. It's your pa, isn't it?' She clutched a kitchen rag in her hand, twisting it in her fingers as she waited for Bannerman to answer her.

'Maggie, Pa is … dead.'

She gasped and shook her head.

Bannerman looked at his sister. 'You didn't tell her?'

She shook her head. 'I didn't want the kids to hear,' she explained apologetically.

'Where are the boys?' Bannerman asked his wife.

'Down at the creek. They should be back any time now.' She dabbed at her eyes with the cloth. 'Jesus help us, Abe. They killed Cecil.' Curtis could tell that the woman's mind was having a hard time believing it. 'What are we going to do?'

'We're going to fight,' Bannerman said curtly. 'We're going to fight hard, and when we're done old Clem

Dawson will wish he'd picked another little town to try to take over.'

'He'll kill us all,' Maggie said. 'Or at least he'll try.'

'He won't succeed,' Curtis said. 'I swear I'll do whatever I have to do to help keep that bastard from running y'all off your land.'

'You see?' Bannerman said to Maggie. 'We've got a little extra help now. Will's good with a gun. He outdrew Evans and shot him dead in a fair gunfight. No one else around Junction City would have had the guts to try that, let alone pull it off. That's why Dawson is panicking.'

Clem Dawson leaned back in the plush chair, carefully toasting the edge of his cigar with a match before fully lighting it. He puffed luxuriantly and released a creamy plume of cigar smoke into the air above his head. He tossed the used match into a metal wastebasket by his chair.

Five men stood across the desk from Dawson. They lingered in uncertain silence, waiting for him to speak. He lifted his eyes and stabbed them at the men, then regarded the tip of his cigar for a moment. Finally, he spoke.

'Where's Mack Kantor?' he said softly.

He liked to speak quietly in moments of tension; it made the men who worked for him listen a little extra carefully.

'He's at the sawbones' place,' one man said. His name was Cal Hamilton and he was one of the newest of

Dawson's hires. He was a large man with a grim visage and, as far as his employer could discern, no sense of humor whatsoever. Not that Dawson cared. He didn't pay them to laugh at his jokes.

And at this moment, he wasn't in a joking mood.

'What kind of shape is he in?'

'His ankle was damn near blowed apart,' Hamilton said. 'Wouldn't be surprised if Doc has to amputate.'

Dawson raised an eyebrow and shook his head.

'A damn shame. Couldn't have happened to a nicer feller.'

Four of the five gunmen smiled at Dawson's joke. Hamilton was the exception.

'And Butch Muller?' Dawson asked.

'Dead,' said Hamilton simply.

Dawson sighed heavily and organized some papers on his desk. He sat back and folded his hands across his stomach.

'This will not stand, gentlemen,' he said, rolling the cigar from one corner of his mouth to the other. 'I pay you all well, I think you'll agree.' He paused. 'Am I right?' He looked from man to man. There were no complaints about compensation. 'In exchange for the wages I pay you, I expect a certain level of professionalism in return. I don't think that's too much to ask. And yet, I seem to be mistaken.' He removed the cigar from his mouth and regarded it for a moment. 'Evidently it is too much to ask, given the carelessness with which Kantor and Muller acted today.'

One of the men appeared like he was going to say something, but a frigid glance from Dawson cut him off.

'Now,' Dawson continued between puffs on his cigar, 'Cecil Bannerman is dead. That makes one of their men for three of mine, if we remember the late Mr Evans. The important thing is that the conflict has now moved out into the open.' He tapped the thick ash off the end of his cigar into an ornate ashtray on the desk. 'We will have to seize the initiative, if you will.'

The office door opened and Alvin Dawson stepped in, his head still bandaged from his encounter with Will Curtis. He closed the door hurriedly and sat down in a leather chair across the room from his father, who gave him a brief stare laced with contempt.

'Mr Hamilton, I have designated you to be the leader for the time being. Your pay will increase according to your level of success.' Hamilton nodded curtly, his features inscrutable. Clem Dawson felt a twinge of irritation at the man's permanent poker face. 'I don't want any mistakes from now on. If you fail, I'm sure one of your ... colleagues will be ready and willing to take over.' He stubbed out his cigar carefully and leaned forward on the desk, his fingers interlaced before him. 'I want you to ride out to Abe Bannerman's place and burn it to the ground. Tonight. I'm not telling you to kill anyone, but if any fools decide to get in your way, then you do what you have to do. Am I clear?'

There was a faint glimmer in Hamilton's eye as the man nodded.

'I have tried to be reasonable with the people in this town, but my attempts have fallen on deaf ears,' said Dawson, examining his fingernails as he spoke. 'If the people around Junction City won't listen to reason, then maybe they'll listen to force. If you pull this off properly, Hamilton, then this will likely be a one-time deal. The homesteaders will see the light and I can start building a real future for this town.' His eyes narrowed as he met Hamilton's gaze. 'Don't let me down.'

'We'll take care of it,' Hamilton said evenly.

Dawson made an impatient gesture.

'All right then, hit the trail. Time is money.'

The gunmen exited through the office door and left the Dawson house. Clem Dawson turned his attention to his son, who sat in silence across the room.

'You made quite a mess, Alvin. I've had to take drastic measures to maintain our family's name.'

'That man insulted me, Pa. And that bitch Sally Bannerman did, too.'

Clem Dawson flinched. 'You know, Alvin, sometimes the sheer depth of your stupidity appalls me.'

A dark crimson color spread from Alvin Dawson's throat up into his cheeks. He clenched his teeth together but lowered his eyes to the carpet. He despised his father, but he feared him even more.

'Here's what you're going to do, Alvin. You're going to go upstairs and get in bed. You need rest to recover from your injury. You're not going to come out for a few days. I don't want you causing any more problems than you already have.' Dawson pushed back his chair and stood up. He was a portly man, with silver hair that was mostly gone on top. His thick mustache was neatly trimmed and combed. 'Just stay out of the way. I'll deal with you soon enough.'

Clem Dawson strode out of the room and his son could hear his footsteps recede down the hallway.

Alvin Dawson remained seated for a few minutes, rage and humiliation coursing through him so powerfully that his chest felt tight. He had felt anger against his father many times before – indeed, more times than he could count. But this was different. This was two humiliations: the one he received from Will Curtis at Bannerman's saloon, and now the command from his father to stay hidden in bed while *real men* cleaned up the mess Alvin had made.

I wouldn't care a bit if the old man died, Alvin Dawson thought. *I wouldn't shed a single tear for that son of a bitch.*

An image flashed through his mind, and part of him recoiled from it. He saw himself standing over his father. Blood trickled from Clem Dawson's mouth, and he cringed in fear of his own son. He saw himself raise a pistol and, ignoring his father's pleas for mercy, fire a shot into the elder Dawson's heart.

He shook his head and scrubbed a hand across his face. Then he climbed upstairs and went back to bed.

CHAPTER FOUR

Will Curtis and Abe Bannerman stood in the darkness of the latter's front porch, smoking cigarettes and talking quietly. Maggie, Sally, and Abe's two young sons had all gone to bed, their moods somber. The shadow of Cecil Bannerman's death was like a dark cloud over the family. Curtis, too, was pensive.

'We're going to have a meeting in the morning at Phil Shirreffs's place,' said Abe Bannerman. He flicked the remains of his cigarette into the darkness beyond the porch. 'We're going to have to get organized.'

'Sally going to stay out here for now?' Curtis asked.

'Yeah. I think that's best.'

'Probably so,' agreed Curtis. 'What about the place in Junction City?'

'I know my pa would've locked up the saloon real careful, so I'm not worried about it right now.'

'Good.' Curtis stifled a yawn. 'I'll take the first watch, like we discussed. You look like you could use some sleep.'

Abe Bannerman rose. In the silvery moonlight, his features were downcast but stoical. He put a hand out toward Will Curtis.

'Thanks for everything,' he said. 'It's probably going to get pretty hairy around here. I'm glad to have your help.'

Curtis rose and gripped Bannerman's hand.

'I'm happy to help. I got a taste of the way Dawson wants to run that town, and I didn't like it.' He hesitated momentarily. 'Also, I'm real sorry about your pa, Abe. I can't pretend to have known him well, but what I did know, I liked.'

Bannerman looked off into the yard, memories of his father crowding his weary mind.

'He was a good man,' he said. 'Always took good care of his family.' He exhaled a breath slowly. 'Anyway, I'll be up in a few hours to take over.'

He went into the house, leaving Will Curtis alone in the cool night air. A light rain began to fall a few seconds later.

Three hours passed. Curtis had made his rounds about the property roughly every thirty minutes. He walked around the cabin itself, scanning the woods around the property as he did so. He walked around the stable and over to the bunkhouse, where the two men who worked for Abe and Maggie Bannerman slept. He could hear them both snoring loudly inside the small building.

There was no sign of anyone lurking in the shadows.

Curtis knew that Abe Bannerman would soon be appearing, ready to take over the watch. He decided to take one last lap around the property before he was relieved. He moved quietly, staying in the dark areas as much as possible.

A cold wind stirred the grass as he passed around the back of the cabin. He was rounding the corner of the bunkhouse when he saw the two men scurry into the trees. His big Navy Colt was in his hand and he aimed where the men had run, firing off three quick shots.

Curtis backed up beneath the eave of the bunkhouse near the woodpile, his eyes scanning the rim of the forest. He heard movement in the bunkhouse and knew his shots had awakened the two ranch hands.

Then he smelled the smoke.

It was coming from the other side of the bunkhouse. His lips tightened. So that's what those two had been doing.

He turned and shouted over his shoulder toward the house.

'Abe! We got a fire out here.'

The door of the bunkhouse burst open and two men came out in their underwear. One had a Winchester in his hands, the other a pistol.

The smoke was thicker now.

Curtis ran toward the back of the bunkhouse, followed by the ranch hands. Flames were swirling across the entire back wall of the building. The fire had already reached the roof and was spreading rapidly. He was relieved that neither man had still been sleeping inside. They would likely have died in the fire before they knew what had happened.

The heat and smoke repelled Curtis and the two others. As he backed away from the fire he noticed the door of the cabin fly open. Abe Bannerman emerged from the house, pulling on a shirt. A pistol was tucked into his waistband. He ran toward Curtis and had nearly reached the back of the bunkhouse when gunfire erupted from the trees beyond.

Curtis swore. They'd been so distracted by the fire that he'd nearly forgotten about the men who'd set it.

The bullets tore into the wall near Curtis, sending shards of wood raining down on his shirt. Both of the ranch hands went down. The older of the two, an elderly man with a long white beard, was clearly dead. The other rolled around on the grass, clutching his abdomen and moaning in agony. Curtis pivoted and stepped toward the fallen cowpunch, despite the bullets hammering into the ground at his feet. He reached out toward the man and had just clutched his arm when a bullet sank into the man's right temple, spurting blood and brain matter across Curtis's shirt. He released the man and followed Abe Bannerman around the building, the roof of which was now completely engulfed in flames.

They raced across the yard away from the bunkhouse. After a short respite, the gunfire once more followed them. Curtis was a feet few behind Bannerman when a bullet blurred past his left shoulder, missing him by no more than an inch. They barely made it to the porch before the full firepower of Dawson's men was unleashed on the cabin. Windows shattered and bullets ricocheted around Curtis and Bannerman as they dived through the door into the dark living room.

The smell of gunsmoke was thick in the air. Bullets pounded into the walls above them.

A voice came to them over the roar of the firing guns. Maggie Bannerman's voice.

'Abe! Are you all right?'

'I'm OK.' Bannerman moved forward on his hands and knees toward the hallway across the room. Will Curtis followed. A stray bullet smashed into a picture on the wall above. It tumbled down, smashing Curtis on his right ear and drawing blood. He ignored the pain until he was safely in the hallway.

On the floor outside one of the bedrooms were Maggie, Sally, and the two young Bannerman boys, Ben and Sam. Abe Bannerman crawled forward and embraced his wife. The bullets kept coming, hammering relentlessly into the cabin.

'Who is it?' Sally Bannerman cried, holding her hands over her ears.

'Dawson's men,' Curtis said. 'No doubt about it.'

'What about the men in the bunkhouse?'

Curtis shook his head soberly. Sally Bannerman understood his meaning.

'The evil bushwhackers,' she said.

Curtis turned to Abe Bannerman and leaned close so that he wouldn't have to yell as loud to be heard.

'You got any ideas? They don't seem like they're going to let up any time soon.'

Bannerman wet his lips with his tongue and looked around the cabin, his face a mask of concentration. He focused on something on the kitchen floor, and Curtis twisted around to see what he was looking at. There was a large rug on the floor there, between the dining table and the wood stove. Curtis turned back to Bannerman, who met his gaze.

The gunfire diminished for a moment, as several of Dawson's men reloaded at the same time.

'I've got a tunnel to my spud cellar,' Bannerman said. He pointed at the rug on the kitchen floor. 'There's a trapdoor under that rug. It leads to the tunnel.'

Curtis frowned. 'When did you put in the tunnel?'

'It was already there when we bought the place,' Bannerman explained. The gunfire had increased again now. 'Never thought I'd be using it to escape from my own house.'

He looked again at the rug, then motioned for Curtis to follow him. They bellied across the floor into the kitchen. A bullet pinged off a skillet hanging on the wall near the stove and both men paused, covering their heads with their hands, before moving on to the rug. Bannerman pulled the edge of the rug back, revealing a plank door in the floor, about three feet square.

Just then the firing stopped entirely. Powdersmoke

drifted on the night air and the sudden silence was eerie. A voice called to them from outside.

'You in there! Listen up and listen good. We know you had something to do with killing Tabor Evans in Junction City. We also know you killed Butch Muller. Come out and have a talk with us. There's been enough killing. We just want to talk.'

Curtis and Bannerman exchanged sardonic glances. Abe Bannerman leaned on one elbow and cupped his hands to his mouth to project his voice.

'Y'all killed my pa,' he called. 'You also killed two of my men out there. Did you forget about that?'

There was a pause before the voice outside responded.

'Either way you look at it, there's been enough killing,' the voice said. 'Let's work this out without any more blood being spilled.'

Bannerman reached out and pulled the latch on the trapdoor, which he swung open, revealing a pitch-black void beneath the floor. The hair bristled on the back of Will Curtis's neck as he pondered crawling through the tunnel. He ignored the anxious sensation when he considered the alternative.

Bannerman called again to the band of killers waiting outside.

'Y'all can rot in hell! Do your best, you bunch of lowdown sidewinders. Anyone who comes close to this house will end up eating lead!'

He looked at Curtis and grinned, then waved the

women and children over into the kitchen. When they reached the trapdoor he reached up and pulled an unlit lantern down from the kitchen table.

'Have it your way, Bannerman,' the voice called from outside. 'That was your last chance to be reasonable.'

A few seconds later the barrage of gunfire erupted again, assailing the cabin anew.

Bannerman handed the lantern to Curtis.

'You go first,' he said. 'Don't light the lantern until you're at least five feet into the tunnel. We don't want anyone outside seeing the light.'

Curtis nodded. The moonlight was sifting through a shattered kitchen window, illuminating the entry into the tunnel a little better. He could see the sturdy-looking wood that helped support it. Whoever had built this tunnel had known what he was doing.

Curtis lowered his feet into the tunnel and then stood up. Only his shoulders and head protruded from the kitchen floor. He took a match from his shirt pocket and knelt down, moving forward into the musty darkness in a crouching position. He had probably gone forward seven or eight feet when he paused, thumb-snapped the lucifer alight, and lit the lantern, keeping the wick turned down low.

When he turned back toward the entrance he could see two legs coming down as the gunfire continued to thunder through the house above him. The legs made the small jump onto the dirt below and Curtis saw Sally Bannerman's nervous face in the dim lamplight. She moved down toward Curtis and was quickly followed by Ben and Sam Bannerman and then their mother.

'They're lighting the house on fire,' Maggie Bannerman said. Her scared eyes glinted in the lantern light.

'Bastards,' said Will Curtis bitterly.

Abe Bannerman dropped into the tunnel and pulled the trapdoor closed above him. Will Curtis turned up the wick on the lantern. He saw two pistols in the waist of Bannerman's pants, and the rancher held a rifle in his hands.

'Let's move,' Curtis said, turning and moving forward on his hands and knees. The others followed closely behind. He could hear them scuffling through the dirt as he crawled. Bright light spilled through the cracks in the trapdoor.

'The house is burning down,' Abe Bannerman said.

Curtis heard Maggie cry out quietly, although she didn't slow down. The crackling sound of burning wood had replaced the sounds of gunfire.

There was a dank smell in the tunnel, and the dirt was a little moist. There was a tight constriction in Curtis's throat, but he powered through his innate claustrophobia, almost irritated with himself for having such a serious physical reaction to the enclosed space. The tunnel seemed endless, and Curtis had to force himself not to ask Abe Bannerman how much further it was to the spud cellar.

'It's not much further, Will,' Bannerman said, as if reading Curtis's mind.

Curtis held the lantern directly in front of his face and saw the end of the tunnel about a dozen yards of ahead of him. He crawled a little faster, eager to reach his destination.

At the end of the tunnel was another trapdoor.

'Go ahead and open it,' Abe Bannerman said. 'But for God's sake be quiet about it.'

Curtis pushed his hands against the trapdoor, which moved up, revealing a small cellar containing several burlap sacks filled with potatoes. Curtis climbed out of the tunnel and reached down to help the others. He had turned down the lantern again.

Abe Bannerman closed the trapdoor after emerging from the tunnel. He and Curtis moved toward the solid wooden door. The walls and ceiling of the cellar were dirt. It appeared to Curtis that they were standing inside a small hill, somewhere on the Bannerman property. He had no idea where he was relative to the house.

Bannerman pulled the door open a couple of inches and Curtis looked out with him. Now he knew where he was. The spud cellar had been built in the side of a tree-covered foothill on the west end of the property. The house was between him and Dawson's men, whose yelling voices carried over the sound of the fire. By this time the entire roof of the cabin was aflame.

'As far as those sons of bitches know, we're all still in there,' said Bannerman, his voice suffused with icy rage.

'They're goddamn child-killers,' Curtis said, shaking his head.

His eyes flicked to the two young boys sitting close to their mother against the far wall of the cellar, then back to the burning house across the yard from him.

Clem Dawson evidently wasn't a man to quibble over minor details like children dying in a fiery inferno. That was clear. And for what? Curtis thought. To be the king of Junction City, a piddly, isolated little town that no one had ever heard of?

A man on a large gelding rode around the cabin, careful to keep his distance from the burning structure. Bannerman stiffened and pushed the cellar door a little more closed. He and Curtis regarded the rider, who was silhouetted against the flames, in silence for a moment. Then the rider finished his lap around the house and disappeared on the other side.

'You got any ideas?' Bannerman asked.

'You got any neighbors nearby?'

Bannerman nodded. 'Phil Shirreffs lives about two miles south of here.'

'Let's send the women and the boys to his place. I take it Maggie knows the way.'

'The boys do, too.'

'Good.' He turned to Sally, who had stepped up behind to the two men. 'Sally, you and Maggie are going to take the boys over the Shirreffs place.'

Sally Bannerman raised an eyebrow.

'What're you two planning to do?' she asked.

'We're going to make these gunslingers wish they'd never heard of Junction City,' said Abe Bannerman.

'What if they kill you?' Sally asked incredulously.

'Ain't going to happen,' Curtis retorted.

'I can shoot as well as either of you,' Sally said. Curtis turned and looked her. 'You think I'm kidding?'

Something about her face brought Curtis up short.

'No, ma'am,' he said. 'I don't think you're kidding.'

Abe Bannerman pulled one of the Colt pistols from his waist and handed it to his sister.

'Sally, you are a damn good shot,' he said. 'That's why I need you to go with Maggie and the boys.' When Sally began to protest, Bannerman held up a hand to quieten dissent. 'What do you think Pa would want you to do?'

Sally's hard glare softened. She looked down at the pistol in her hand, which was trembling slightly.

'All right, Abe,' she said. 'You win.'

'There's a first time for everything,' Bannerman said with quiet exultation. Curtis and Sally smiled, grateful for at least one moment of levity.

'I won't let it happen again, you can bet on that,' Sally said.

Bannerman waved his wife and children over.

'Y'all are going over to Phil Shirreffs's place,' he said. 'Sally has a pistol.'

'What about you two?'

'Don't worry about us. We're going to be careful. You know that.'

'I know,' Maggie said. Abe patted his boys on their heads. 'Boys, you take care of your mother and your

Aunt Sally, y'hear?'

'Sure, Pa,' said Ben Bannerman. Curtis figured the boys were eight and ten years old, or thereabouts. They looked like serious boys.

Curtis peered through the doorway, his shoulder throbbing. He saw men on horseback pull reins on the side of the house, sinister in the firelight. One reached into a saddlebag and removed a bottle. He used his teeth to remove the cork, which he spat toward the flames. He drank deeply, then passed the bottle to his friend. Neither looked toward the spud cellar.

'Those fellers ain't from around here,' Abe Bannerman observed. 'They don't know about this cellar.' He looked at his wife and his sister. 'Y'all ready?' They nodded and he turned the lampwick almost entirely down as Curtis opened the door.

A few birch trees stood not far from the cellar door. They obscured the movements of the women and the children as they exited the cellar and moved off in darkness toward the forest beyond the edge of the yard.

They were stealthy and silent in their movements. The two horsemen continued to pass the whiskey bottle back and forth, oblivious to the movements in the trees. One of them tossed the empty bottle into the house just as the roof collapsed. The riders laughed uproariously and heeled their mounts back toward the barn.

Curtis and Bannerman made their move. They catfooted out through the door, closing it behind them. They moved into the trees to their right and used the cover of the dark forest to move around to the other side of the yard, between the bunkhouse and the barn. Here they had a complete view of the front of the incinerated house.

Curtis was relieved that the buildings were far enough apart for the barn not to have caught fire. He could hear the horses stirring in their stalls, terrified by the sounds of the gunfire and the smell of the smoke.

Bannerman handed his last remaining pistol to Curtis, keeping the Winchester for himself. He levered a bullet into the chamber.

There were five men in the yard, all mounted. Each had a rifle in his scabbard and a pistol strapped to his hip. They were sitting their horses, staring at the fire.

By now they must think everyone in the cabin had been killed, either by a bullet or by the fire, Curtis thought. He noticed that they almost looked bored by the entire process. This was not their first time killing people, he thought, or burning down houses. When Dawson hired gunmen, he chose real professionals.

'You take the two on the left,' Curtis said tightly, thumbing back the hammer on his Navy Colt. 'I'll take the three on the right.'

CHAPTER FIVE

Will Curtis and Abe Bannerman aimed carefully. Because they hadn't been spotted by Dawson's men, they took their time and made their bullets count.

Bursts of orange flame erupted from the muzzles of their guns as they fired. Although it was an unspoken agreement, both men were shooting to kill. The horsemen across the yard from them were hired killers who had just attempted to massacre an entire family – for money. As far as they knew, they had succeeded. They had chosen their line of work, and now they would take the consequences of their actions.

Their first shots blasted two of the gunmen out of their saddles. They collapsed forward, face-planting onto the ground with the solidity of dead weight.

Curtis's second shot was a miss due to the startled horses of the three remaining killers. Bannerman connected, however, hitting the middle rider in the back of the neck. The rider tumbled sideways out of the saddle and his horse reared, pawing at the air in terror before breaking into a run toward the trees across the yard. The man's left foot remained stuck in the stirrup, and he screamed as the horse dragged him like a rag doll into the shadows.

'What the hell?' the gunman on the left hollered, hipping in the saddle and looking toward Curtis and Bannerman's position. His hand streaked toward his pistol, but before he could clear leather his body jerked as one of Curtis's bullets tore into his collarbone. He gasped and leaned forward, clutching the saddle horn and trying to steady himself. He reached again for his gun but was cut down by a bullet that penetrated his skull just above his right ear. He crashed from the saddle onto the ground, further propelled by his fleeing horse.

Only one of the Dawson men remained. He neck-reined his horse and looked toward Curtis. For a moment the cowboy thought the man was looking right into his eyes, although he knew that wasn't possible. Curtis raised his pistol toward the gunman, but before he could fire he heard the report of Bannerman's Winchester from a few feet away. A large chunk of the brim of the horseman's hat flew off and drifted toward the grass.

The man dug his spurs deeply into his horse's ribs, sending the animal into a panicky, full-speed gallop away from the cabin and toward the forest. He disappeared through a dense plume of black smoke that was drifting across the yard from the burning cabin. No longer able to get a shot off, Curtis lowered his gun and looked toward the three unmoving shapes scattered across the Bannermans' yard. They were well illuminated in the light of the fire.

It was less than an hour later when Curtis and Bannerman rode into Phil Shirreffs's yard. Dawn had appeared above the tree-cloaked ridges that surrounded the property.

Shirreffs was standing on his porch sipping a cup of coffee. His expression was serious as he greeted the two riders.

'Morning, Abe.' He nodded at Curtis. 'Will.'

'Morning, Phil,' said Bannerman as he and Curtis dismounted. They tied their horses to a pole near the porch. 'I'm sure Sally and Maggie have filled you in.'

'They have. They're all asleep inside.' He lowered his voice a little. 'Did you fellers manage to turn the tables on Dawson's boys?'

Curtis smiled thinly. 'We got four out of five of 'em.'

'Good to hear that,' said Shirreffs. 'What're we all going to do next?'

Bannerman folded his arms and leaned against the porch rail. Curtis removed the makings from his pocket and began to build a smoke.

'I think y'all are going to have to take the fight to Dawson,' Curtis said as he twisted the end of his cigarette. 'You can be sure that he'll plan on killing anyone who stands in his way now. He's going to be real ornery when he hears how many of his hired guns bit the dust.'

Shirreffs glanced at Bannerman.

'What do you think, Abe?'

'I don't see how we have any other choice,' Bannerman replied. 'Unless you call getting run out of our homes a choice.'

'I don't.'

'Didn't think so. But Dawson's playing for keeps, Phil.'

'I can see that,' Shirreffs said thoughtfully. His eyes regarded Curtis appraisingly. 'You sure you want to get all mixed up in this?'

'I ain't got nothing else going on right now,' said Curtis in a relaxed tone. 'Once Tabor Evans pulled that gun on me, I decided to take a special interest in Clem Dawson.' He took a long drag on his cigarette. 'Not to mention his chickenshit son.'

Bannerman chuckled. 'That Alvin makes me want to retch. I've heard that even his own pa can hardly stand him.'

Curtis raised his head. 'That right?'

'Yeah, I've heard that, too,' Shirreffs added. 'Heard his pa bit the kid's head off in the bank in front of a whole bunch of folks a while back.'

'Maybe that's why Alvin likes his whiskey so much,' said Curtis.

'What do you mean when you say we should bring the fight to Dawson?' Shirreffs asked.

Curtis frowned. 'He's vulnerable right now,' he said.

'Almost every one of his bushwhackers is dead. He won't have had time to call in any reinforcements yet.' He smiled faintly. 'It might be a good time for one of us to pay a visit to Mr Dawson.'

'He's still got one gunslinger working for him,' Bannerman said.

'I know,' Curtis said. 'I can handle him, though.'

'So you're volunteering?' Shirreffs asked.

'Yeah, I guess I am. I know where Dawson lives. Sally showed me after I met Alvin Dawson and Tabor Evans.'

'You're going to need some help,' Bannerman said.

Curtis shook his head.

'Not for this chore I don't. Dawson won't be expecting it. That'll make my job that much easier.' He glanced toward the door of Shirreffs's house. 'You don't need to take any unnecessary risks.'

'What do you have in mind?'

A cunning smile tugged at the corner of Curtis's lips.

'Well, I was thinking I would ride into town tonight ...'

It was a foggy night, with intermittent rain. Junction City was immersed in darkness when Will Curtis halted his horse in the alley behind Sally Bannerman's saloon.

He tied his horse to a pole by the back door and stood in the shadows, watching and listening. His eyes scanned the rutted alleyway for any signs of movement. After a few minutes he was satisfied that no one had seen him.

Curtis was glad Junction City was a small town without much in the way of nightlife. Now its sole saloon was closed and the streets were virtually deserted. Peering down the alley toward the south end of town, he saw no signs of life. He turned and started walking in the direction of Clem Dawson's house.

He had removed his spurs and left them in his saddlebag. He didn't want them chiming and betraying his approach to anyone who might be looking for him. His right hand gripped the butt of his Navy Colt, ready to swing it into action at the first sign of danger. But there were no such signs, even as he came upon the back yard of the Dawson residence.

He took cover behind a large apple tree at the rear left corner of the yard. His breathing was shallow and his heart pounded in his chest. The yard was well maintained, with rose bushes and neatly trimmed grass. A thick tangle of ivy climbed up the back of the house, showing clearly in the moonlight.

Curtis was patient. He knew Dawson still had one man left, and he figured that man was somewhere out here in the night air, waiting and watching just as Curtis was. After almost five minutes, however, he was beginning to question that assumption. Nothing stirred in the darkness behind Dawson's house. From where Curtis was standing, he could see the entire north side of the house and part of the front yard. He saw no movement there, either.

What if the last of Dawson's gunmen had skipped

town? Curtis thought. Maybe he'd been so scared by seeing Dawson's other men shot down that he'd lit out. This had turned into a more dangerous job than the man had anticipated, Curtis was sure. Men had abandoned jobs for less.

Curtis had just taken a step toward the back porch when he heard a cough. A tingle snaked down his spine and he hastily moved back behind the tree. He unconsciously loosened his pistol in its holster, all his senses attuned to the danger he sensed.

He tried to get an idea of where the cough had come from, his eyes piercing the pools of darkness around the yard. There was a large laurel bush near the back steps of the house. Curtis was watching it closely when he heard another cough. It was coming from behind the bush, which was well over six feet high.

Curtis fixed his eyes on the bush and tensed. A man moved out from behind the bush and paused near the steps. He was a big man with a cruel face. He scratched a finger along his jawline and moved his gaze around the yard. His glance passed over Curtis, who held his breath and rested his thumb on the hammer of his pistol. To his relief, he hadn't been spotted in the darkness beneath the apple tree, and the man continued scanning the rest of the large back yard with the dark eyes that looked to Curtis like bullet holes.

When he had finished looking the yard over, the man started walking toward the outhouse, which was located about ten feet from the tree behind which

Curtis stood. Curtis examined the man closely. He was wearing a black trench coat and a big brown Stetson. Curtis noticed that a large chunk of the brim on the right side of the hat was missing. He knew exactly where the man's hat had been damaged.

Sure that he hadn't been seen, Curtis watched the man open the outhouse door and step inside. It was a few minutes before the man emerged, wiping his hands on the legs of his pants. He carefully closed the door behind him and was turning back to his position behind the laurel bush when Curtis stepped out from behind the tree, his pistol fixed on the gunman. The man froze.

'Hands up,' Curtis said softly. The man hesitated and Curtis knew what he was thinking. 'You'd better be real sure before you make a move. 'Cause I'm sure – you can bet on that.' Moonlight reflected off the barrel of Curtis's gun.

The man cast a murderous glare at Curtis and slowly raised his hands.

'Higher,' Curtis commanded, his voice still quiet but menacing. The man obeyed.

Curtis gestured toward the shadows behind the apple tree.

'Git,' he said. The man walked cautiously toward Curtis, who waved the pistol further into the darkness. 'Couple more feet.' The man moved forward, the tree blocking any possible view of the exchange from within the Dawson house.

'What's your name?' Curtis asked.

'Cal Hamilton.'

'You picked the wrong man to work for, Cal Hamilton,' Curtis said. Hamilton's mouth twisted into a smirk, and Curtis's anger intensified. 'Don't believe me? Ask your four friends. You know – the ones you left in the yard out at Abe Bannerman's place.' The smirk left Hamilton's lips. 'Boy, you rode out of there real fast like, Cal Hamilton. I wouldn't be surprised if you shit your pants on the way.'

Hamilton's face was harsh as his eyes bore into Curtis's. Curtis had no doubt that, if he could, Cal Hamilton would have blown him away right there where they stood.

'Pull your pistol and toss it on the ground, Cal Hamilton. You ain't going to need it any more tonight.'

Hamilton hesitated again. Curtis decided the man needed a little encouragement.

Before Hamilton knew what was happening, Curtis took a swift step toward him, swinging the heavy pistol up into the man's throat. Hamilton tumbled backward, gasping for breath and clawing at his throat. His trench coat fell open, revealing the ivory-handled Remington pistol inside the killer's fancy embroidered holster.

The fingers on Hamilton's right hand twitched and he made a move toward the weapon, his left hand still clutched at his neck. Curtis threw himself atop the man, thrusting his knee hard into Hamilton's chest and pressing the barrel of the Navy Colt against his nose, which bent and flattened awkwardly against his face.

'Just try it, friend,' Curtis hissed through his teeth, leaning in close. 'You tried to kill an entire family last night. You think I forgot that?'

Hamilton's eyes were wide with fear. He threw his arms out to show that he was no threat to Curtis.

'It wasn't my idea,' he said as he grimaced in pain. 'Honest. I didn't know they were going to light the cabin on fire.'

Curtis snorted with disdain. 'Yellow-bellied, lyin' dry-gulcher. You make me sick. You knew exactly what was going to happen. You just didn't figure we'd get the drop on you. I guess your dead buddies didn't figure on that either, did they?'

Hamilton was silent, warily watching Curtis, whose anger seemed to overflow from within him. Curtis's finger was on the trigger and the hammer was pulled back. Hamilton could feel his hot breath in his face. He was fairly sure that Curtis was going to kill him, right there by the apple tree in Clem Dawson's back yard.

Curtis struggled to tame the killing urge within him. He realized he was clenching his teeth so tightly that it hurt. He could see the naked fear in Hamilton, even though the man's face was partially obscured in shadow.

He reminded himself that he had come into Junction City this night to fulfill a task. If he shot Cal Hamilton here he would undoubtedly awaken anyone in Dawson's house, and probably several of the man's neighbors as well.

Curtis relaxed his jaw and some of the tension seemed to leave his body. He slowly put the hammer back down, and Hamilton exhaled with audible relief.

'Don't go celebrating quite yet, Hamilton,' said Curtis.

He swiftly raised the pistol away from Hamilton's head and then brought it down hard, cracking the gunman across the left side of his skull. The skin split and blood began to flow freely down Hamilton's neck and into his shirt. Hamilton's eyes rolled back in his head and his body went limp.

Curtis dragged him a little further back into the darkness and removed some pre-cut lengths of rope from the pocket of his sheepskin coat. He bound the unconscious man at the wrists and ankles, then stuffed a handkerchief into his mouth and tied another one around his face, gagging him.

He dragged Hamilton behind the outhouse, where he dropped him in some bushes. Then he turned and strode purposefully toward the back door of Clem Dawson's house.

He climbed the steps carefully. They didn't creak beneath his feet. He paused momentarily and looked back toward the outhouse. There was no movement in the bushes where he'd deposited Cal Hamilton.

Curtis tested the doorknob and was surprised when the door opened, revealing a dark kitchen beyond. His earlier supposition had been correct: Clem Dawson wasn't expecting anyone to make a move on him in his own house. Either that or he still had a lot of unwarranted confidence in Cal Hamilton's abilities. Whatever the case, Dawson's laxity had made Curtis's job much easier.

Curtis stepped through the door and closed it quietly behind him. He waited for his eyes to adjust. Pale moonlight spilled into the room through a large window near the stove. The kitchen was large and very clean. He could discern no sounds of movement within the house. He leaned down and removed his boots, tucking them under his left arm as he drew his pistol with his right hand.

He moved around the large cutting table in the middle of the kitchen and entered the hallway, where he again paused before continuing on toward the front of the house. There was no one in the parlor or the living room. A lantern burned dimly in Dawson's office beyond, on the other side of the living room. No one was in the office. There was a closed door across the hall from the parlor entrance. Curtis figured it was the maid's room; he listened at the door for a minute but heard nothing inside.

He moved toward the stairway in the hall. The steps had a thick carpet on them and Curtis smiled, glad that Dawson was so dedicated to comfort in his home. He climbed the steps noiselessly and peered around the wall into the dark hallway on the second floor. Three doors opened off the hallway; two on the right and one on the left.

The door on the left had to be Clem Dawson's, Curtis decided.

He stepped to the door and reached for the knob. He had barely touched it when the door slid open a few inches. Curtis couldn't believe that Dawson was sleeping with his bedroom door unlocked, let alone ajar. Suspicious now, he dragged his pistol from leather and leaned forward, peering into the dim room.

A lantern was turned down low on the end table beside Dawson's bed. A pistol lay beside the lantern on the table. Curtis's eyes swiveled to the bed. He could see a shape lying there. It was the bulky shape of Clem Dawson, sleeping deeply. Curtis could hear the slow rhythm of Dawson's breathing.

He watched the sleeping man for a moment, then entered the room, closing the door softly behind him. There was no change in Dawson's slumber. His right hand still held the pistol, which he held out toward Clem Dawson. For all he knew, the man had another gun hidden under his pillow. Curtis wasn't taking any chances. If Dawson tried any gunplay, he'd be dead before he could do any damage.

Curtis made his move. Within seconds, he had crossed the room and was standing beside Dawson. He lifted his Colt and brought it down as hard as he could onto Dawson's pasty right ankle, which protruded from the silk sheets.

Curtis could feel the crack of metal against bone. Dawson was suddenly wide awake, his eyes bulging. He opened his mouth to scream but Curtis moved forward and clamped his strong, rough hand over the lower part of the banker's face, stifling any cries. Curtis raised his Colt and pressed the end of the muzzle against Dawson's cheek. He leaned forward and spoke quietly.

'This would be a very bad time for you to scream,' he said menacingly. 'It could be bad for your health.'

Dawson nodded quickly.

'You're not a very nice man,' Curtis continued. 'I guess you think you own this town, don't you?' Dawson didn't respond, but kept his fearful eyes on Curtis's. 'You're going to learn a lesson, Dawson. You shouldn't have played around with the Bannermans or their neighbors. Are you starting to understand that?'

He pressed the muzzle deeper into Dawson's cheek, making an indentation in the man's thick flesh. 'You're going to pay for what you did to Cecil Bannerman. Only a lowdown yellow snake would hire gunslingers to do his dirty work for him.' He leaned in closer toward Dawson's face. 'You tried to kill Abe Bannerman and his entire family. Two little kids, Dawson. They'd have been burnt alive in that cabin. And why? What do the Bannermans have that you want?'

The reptilian eyes regarded Curtis, who pulled his hand away from Dawson's mouth to allow the man to answer the question. Curtis kept the muzzle in his face.

'You got it all wrong, Curtis,' said Dawson, his oily voice low. 'I never wanted Cecil dead. Those men did it without my authorization.'

'Why?' Curtis demanded skeptically.

'Because of Evans. He was their friend. They wanted revenge. I tried to call them off, but they wouldn't listen to reason.'

Curtis hesitated. 'Why didn't you contact the law in Eugene?'

'I want to, believe you me. But Hamilton won't let me out of his sight. He's obsessed with killing you now. He was hiding out there somewhere in the yard, waiting for you.'

'Yeah, I know. He's taking a nap in the bushes as we speak.'

'Please, Curtis. That's your name, isn't it?' Curtis didn't answer the question. 'Let me go, will you? I'll prove I'm not behind all the violence that's been going on.'

'How?'

Before Dawson could answer, Curtis's ears pricked at the sound of a footfall in the hallway behind him. He turned his head just slightly and Dawson pounced, grabbing the barrel of the gun. He attempted to twist it out of Curtis's hand, bending Curtis's finger painfully.

Curtis smashed his left fist into Dawson's eye, forcing the man to release the gun. Dawson cried out in pain. Curtis turned on the bed and pointed his pistol at the door just as someone pushed it open from the hallway.

A gun blasted from the doorway before Curtis had time to fire. A slug slammed into the wall above Curtis's head. He ducked, spinning off the bed as he triggered a shot toward the door. The man in the doorway screamed and doubled over, then collapsed onto the rug.

Curtis leapt to his feet and looked toward Clem Dawson, who was reaching desperately for the gun on his nightstand. He grabbed it and hoisted it toward Curtis, who fired from the hip without aiming and made a lucky shot, striking Dawson in his outstretched wrist. The gun flew from his hand and landed on the floor near Curtis's feet. Dawson clutched his arm and rolled into a fetal position, sobbing with pain and fear. Curtis kicked the pistol across the room and it disappeared beneath a large wardrobe near the window.

Curtis stared at Clem Dawson for a moment, rage swirling within him. He had never shot an unarmed man in his life, but he had to struggle mightily to keep himself from sending a bullet straight between Clem Dawson's eyes.

Boots pounded up the staircase, inadvertently saving Dawson's life.

A large shape filled the doorway.

'Curtis!' the shape yelled.

They had only spoken briefly, but Curtis recognized the voice of Cal Hamilton. How in hell had the man gotten loose? Curtis wondered. His mind went blank as Hamilton lifted his Remington and fired, narrowly missing Curtis's head. He heard the click as Hamilton's thumb pulled back the hammer for another shot. Raising his pistol, he fanned the hammer of his own gun with lightning speed, sending the rest of his bullets into Hamilton's silhouette before the killer could get off another shot.

Hamilton's body jerked and then fell like a pole-axed steer, directly on top of the other man on the floor. Neither gunman moved.

Noise from the bed attracted Curtis's attention. He turned his head and a bullet whizzed by him. Dawson was clutching a small pistol in his left hand. The drawer to his nightstand was open, and Curtis realized he must have kept a second pistol in it.

Dawson raised the weapon and fired again. The shot was wild, missing Curtis entirely. Curtis moved toward the bed with the intention of taking the weapon away from Dawson. Before the cowpunch could reach him Dawson fired again, and this time his shot was on target. It hit Curtis in the left side of his ribcage and passed through his back, sending him hurtling back against the wall. A thick streak of blood smudged the wall as Curtis slid down toward the floor.

Emboldened, Dawson steadied the weapon with his bloody right hand and squeezed off another shot, which hit the floor a few feet away from Curtis. For a moment, Curtis considered trying for one of the guns of the two prostrate men near the doorway, but this would leave him exposed to Dawson. Using every ounce of strength remaining to him, he heaved himself away from the wall and dived into the hallway. A bullet followed him, striking the door of the bedroom opposite that of Clem Dawson.

Curtis could hear Dawson moving off the bed and shuffling after him. He pulled himself to his feet and made for the stairs. Dawson sent yet another bullet after him, but Curtis had already descended the stairs and was making for the back door by that time. Adrenaline pushed him forward, despite the serious pain and bleeding in his upper abdomen. He crashed through the back door of Dawson's house and ran awkwardly down the alley in the direction of Bannerman's saloon.

He was out of the city limits within sixty seconds of mounting his horse. He had left his boots on Clem Dawson's bedroom floor.

CHAPTER SIX

Two days later fear came to Junction City. It looked like it had come to stay.

There were ten men this time, all bearing the unmistakable aura of the professional killer. Each bore a badge, too – the badge of a deputy sheriff of Lane County. Word had it that Clem Dawson had paid big money to have these men deputized. Everyone knew he had a lot of connections at all levels of government in the state of Oregon.

Weeks passed.

Dawson was taking no chances this time. His right arm was still in a sling from the bullet Will Curtis had sent through his wrist. Everywhere he went he was accompanied by three of the 'deputies' he'd brought to town. Every weekday residents would see him walk to the bank in the morning and then return home in the evening, three large, dark-visaged men walking with him, their eyes scanning the buildings around them. Two other guards were on permanent watch at the Dawson residence. The others patrolled the streets in shifts, looking for any sign of the local homesteaders who were opposing Dawson. The banker hadn't sent the gunmen into the hills to retaliate. Yet.

His son, Alvin, was bedridden, paralysed by another bullet fired by Curtis. The sawbones told Dawson that Alvin would never walk again. Although he never verbalized his feelings, Alvin Dawson bitterly regretted having taken his pistol and trying to defend his father that night. Where had it got him? A life sentence as an invalid. His father had never thanked him for the sacrifice Alvin had made on his behalf.

There was no dissent in Junction City. Local residents had been frightened of Dawson before, but now there was no question that it was his town, and that they would abide by his rules.

In the meantime, Clem Dawson was busy making plans. He knew Will Curtis was still around, hiding somewhere up in the hills among the recalcitrant homesteaders. The ranchers and farmers in the area were now united in their opposition to Dawson. Those who had wavered in the past about selling their land to him now stood firm. They wouldn't sell, no matter what the offer was.

It was now a battle of wills, and might.

But if there was one thing Clem Dawson believed, it was that every man has his price. His experiences in business and politics had taught him that, time and time again. So he planned his strategy, unworried by the opposition in the hills.

Because he had found a man – one of the homesteaders – and that man had named his price. He really had no choice.

Dawson set his plan into motion on a frosty night in late November.

Will Curtis had lost so much blood after Clem Dawson shot him that he almost didn't make it out to Phil Shirreffs's spread that night. It had taken the dedicated ministrations of both Sally and Maggie Bannerman to pull him through, along with some help from Abe Bannerman himself, who had some experience with dressing wounds.

Shirreffs had let the Bannermans and Curtis stay in his bunkhouse for a few days, and then the family had moved out to their uncle's ranch, taking Curtis with them. Abe and Maggie had decided against building a new house out at their own property. They had salvaged what they could from the charred ruins and taken it back with them to their new home.

The shot had taken out a chunk of the bottom rib on Curtis's left side. The bullet had passed through his back, somehow missing any vital organs. Curtis had slept for much of the first week after getting shot. It was early in the second week when he got up and began walking around, slowly building up his strength again. His appetite returned and at the end of the second week he began spending an hour every day at target practice, shooting tin cans off the fence at the edge of the property. A day or two later he rode his horse again for the first time.

There was a flinty determination in Will Curtis now. The women noticed it, and so did Abe Bannerman. The local homesteaders had set up patrols of their own. They rode in shifts at night, vigilant against any attacks by Clem Dawson's men. They had no doubt that the attack would come, sooner or later. Their only defense was to be prepared, and to meet fire with fire when hostilities finally did erupt out in the open. They travelled by secret trails known only to the homesteaders themselves. Shirreffs's house was the headquarters for patrollers. Curtis was determined to be part of those patrols as soon as he possibly could.

One afternoon Abe Bannerman rode into his yard after attending a meeting at Phil Shirreffs's place. He dismounted and looked past the corral. Will Curtis was there, diligently shooting at his tin cans. Bannerman watched him for a few minutes. At first when he started his shooting regimen, Curtis's aim had been shaky, albeit still better than that of most of the ranchers in the Junction City area.

Now it was more than improved – it was better than it had ever been. Over and over, Curtis knocked every can off the fence. Then he would set them up and repeat the process from various distances and positions. Bannerman thought that every time he shot a can Curtis was seeing the face of Clem Dawson.

That night over supper Curtis announced his

readiness to take part in the patrols. Abe Bannerman looked at him from across the table. He dipped a roll in some gravy and chewed thoughtfully before responding.

'We'll be glad to have you, Will,' he said. 'We need every man we can get.'

That night Curtis joined Bannerman on a four-hour watch. They roamed the hills in and around the properties of their neighbors, taking care to stay away from the main trails. Every night there were at least three riders in the hills, sometimes four. They were looking for Dawson's gunmen, but there had been no sign of them so far. That was true on Curtis's first night, too.

Bannerman and Curtis discussed it as they rode home through the woods.

'What do you think, Will?' Bannerman asked.

'He's got something up his sleeve,' said Curtis. 'He's biding his time. Maybe he's in worse shape physically than we thought.'

Bannerman shook his head.

'I just don't know. But something's going to happen soon. I can feel it.'

Abe Bannerman's hunch turned out to be right.

It was the night after Curtis's first patrol when someone torched the Bannermans' saloon, which had been unused since the night Curtis had ridden into town. The fire started around midnight. There was no rain, and there hadn't been for three days. There was very little moisture to impede the flames.

The citizens of Junction City turned out to battle the fire. Thanks to their combined efforts they were able to prevent the fire from spreading to the hardware store next door to the saloon. Several of Dawson's gunmen stood by impassively, watching the saloon burn without making any attempt to help put out the fire.

It was the opening salvo in Clem Dawson's war against the Bannermans and Will Curtis. They were his focus now, although he had no love for the other homesteaders in the area.

Dawson had hoped that burning the saloon down would smoke out Bannerman and Curtis. It didn't work. Dawson was compelled to implement his secondary plan.

Jake Douglas rode out to the Bannermans' cabin the next morning and told them about the burning of the saloon. No one had any doubt about who was responsible for the arson.

'I'm surprised he didn't do it sooner,' said Abe Bannerman cynically. 'I didn't want you trying to run that place by yourself anyway, Sally. With Pa gone, it's just not a place for a young woman.'

Sally Bannerman dabbed her eyes with a handkerchief.

'I know you're right, Abe,' she said. 'Still – that place meant so much to Pa.'

'Junction City's not the same place it used to be. Pa didn't want to accept that, but it's true. Since Clem

Dawson came to town it's become an ugly place.'

'He did this to test us,' Will Curtis said. He glanced at Abe Bannerman. 'He's hoping this will bring us into town. He's got a trap set, of course.'

'Knowing Dawson, I don't doubt it.'

'He brought all those hardcases to town. I guess he wants them to earn their keep.'

The Bannerman boys came out and joined their father in the yard.

'Where y'all going?' Sally asked.

'We left a few things in the barn at our old place,' said Bannerman. 'We're going to take the wagon and make a clean sweep.'

'You need my help?' asked Curtis.

'No, we can handle it. 'Sides, I'd feel better knowing you're here with Maggie and Sally.'

'All right with me,' Curtis said. He took a sip of the strong black coffee that Maggie Bannerman made every morning when the family rose just after dawn.

Bannerman and his sons went into the barn and emerged presently with the wagon. Curtis and Sally waved as they passed the house.

'Be back in a few hours,' Abe Bannerman called.

Curtis sat down on the steps. He gazed at the dewy grass in the yard. Sally sat down beside him and gathered her skirt around her legs.

'How're you doing, Will?' she asked after a time. She turned her head toward him. He kept his eyes on the grass.

'I'm fine.'

'You sure?'

'Yeah, I'm sure.' He laughed quietly. 'Why did you ask it like that?'

She shrugged. 'I don't know. You seem so serious lately. I guess I was a little worried.'

'Well, we're dealing with serious business here.'

Now it was her turn to laugh.

'You don't have to tell me that,' she said.

'I know. Sorry.'

He drank more coffee, draining his cup. He put the empty cup down on the step between him and Sally.

'What're your plans, Will?'

'I'm going to help Abe with some things around here after him and the boys get back.'

'No – I mean your long-term plans.'

'To be honest, I don't really know. I'm going to see this through. Haven't really considered what I'm going to do after that. If I'm still alive that is.' His attempt at humor fell flat.

'You like Junction City?' she asked.

He raised an eyebrow and looked at her. She met his gaze without wavering.

'I like *you*,' he said. 'I still haven't made up my mind about Junction City. You can't blame me there.'

She pushed a strand of hair out of her eyes.

'No, I can't. It hasn't exactly been hospitable to you.'

'It hasn't treated you too well either,' Curtis said. 'You ever thought about leaving?'

'No,' she said firmly. 'I grew up here. I could never leave as long as Abe, Maggie, and the boys are here.'

Curtis hid his disappointment. 'I can understand that,' he said.

'Where were you before?' she asked. 'I mean, I know you came from Idaho originally ...'

'I've been all around the Western states. Wyoming, Colorado, Nevada, Idaho, California, Oregon. Lived my first fifteen years in Idaho. After that, I did a lot of drifting.'

'How'd you make a living?'

'Mostly punching cows. Did some farming here and there, but never really had the stomach for it.'

'The way you've helped around here, we thought maybe you'd been a lawman or something like that.'

Curtis's face darkened.

'I have done a little law work,' he said. 'Nothing official. Got involved in a murder investigation in eastern Oregon a couple of years ago. Ended up almost getting me killed. I figured that was enough badge-toting for me.'

'I think you'd be good at it,' she said. She straightened out the edge of her skirt. 'Still, I can see how it could bring a man down, seeing all the ugly things a sheriff or a marshal has to see.'

'I'd never seen anything like what I saw over in Fillmore. People killing entire families, including little kids.'

'Terrible.'

'Yes, it was. I never thought I'd see anything like that again, till I came here.'

'I guess there're bad folks everywhere.'

'Yes,' he said, troubled by the memories. 'There certainly are.'

They were quiet for a time, watching two horses drinking from a trough in the corral.

'You know, you could make a real nice life for yourself here, Will,' she said pensively.

'You think?'

'Yes, I do. I mean, Clem Dawson isn't going to be in power here for ever. Not with you and my brother and the other ranchers opposing him like you are.'

'Sally, he's hired professional gunmen. They don't play by the same kind of rules that me and Abe do.'

'I know that,' she said.

'Guys like Shirreffs and Wilson – they can shoot and they've got guts. But it will take more than that to finish off Dawson.'

'You sound like you don't think it can be done.' Her voice was soft, and Curtis realized that he was discouraging her.

'Now, Sally, I don't want you to go off getting that idea.'

'It's just—'

'No, no,' he said. 'Dawson ain't licked us yet. Not by a long shot. We ain't going to let that happen, let me tell you.'

He placed his hand on her shoulder and her face

turned to his.

'Do you mean that?' she asked plaintively. 'After all, they killed my father. This is all so much for me to take in.'

'I know it is,' he said. 'If I didn't think we had a chance, I'd tell you. I swear I would.'

'I believe you.'

'I just want you to understand that it ain't going to be an overnight thing. And it's going to take some luck along the way, too.'

Suddenly she leaned over and kissed him. He was startled by it, but a feeling of happiness and exhilaration came over him.

'You do what you have to do,' she said. 'I'll support you all the way.'

With that, she rose and walked back into the cabin.

Late at night, ten days after the burning of the saloon, Curtis rode over to Phil Shirreffs's homestead. He was going to meet Jake Douglas and John Wilson there. With Shirreffs, they would take the patrol for the night.

Abe Bannerman had showed Curtis all the back trails in the hills outside Junction City. Curtis took one of those isolated back trails to Shirreffs's place. The wind moved through the bare branches of the maple trees above him as his sorrel picked its way up an incline. The animal's ears perked up and it lifted its eyes toward the trees up ahead on the right.

Curtis pulled reins and moved to the side of the trail.

His Navy Colt was in his hand and he thumbed back the hammer. Minutes passed, then he decided to proceed, but cautiously. He had gone no more than twenty yards when he heard the sound of movement in the branches where his horse had looked before. He raised his Colt.

'You got about three seconds to show yourself or I'm going to start firing,' Curtis said in a loud voice.

Moments later a man rolled awkwardly out of the trees onto the trail. He had a pistol in his hand. There were dry, crushed leaves on his clothing and his hat was askew on his head. Curtis realized the man had slipped and slid down the side of the hill, revealing his position.

The man watched Curtis. He didn't raise his gun, because he was already looking down the barrel of Curtis's weapon. There was fear and a certain amount of confusion in the man's face. As Curtis watched him an empty whiskey bottle rolled down from the trees where the man had been hiding. It smacked up against one of the man's boots.

'Who're you?' Curtis demanded.

The man hesitated.

'Name's Ike Gibson,' he said. His eyes were bright from the liquor he'd consumed.

'That right?' Curtis asked sarcastically. 'All right, Ike Gibson, what the hell are you doing hiding in the woods with a pistol?'

Gibson cleared his throat, his mind groping for an explanation.

'I – uh – I'm a cousin of Jake Douglas.'

'Yeah?'

'I was riding out to his place. Haven't seen him in a few years.'

Curtis's eyes narrowed. 'Why you taking this trail to get out to Jake's?' he asked.

'I heard there's been some trouble 'round Junction City. I didn't want to run into anybody who was … unfriendly, if you know what I mean.'

'That why you were hiding in the trees?'

Ike Gibson smiled sheepishly.

'Yeah. Didn't know if you were one of the hired guns I heard about. I don't want any trouble, just want to see my cousin.'

Curtis sat for a few moments, considering the man before him and the explanations he'd given. *There's one way to find out if he really is Jake's cousin,* he thought.

'Well, I'm heading to a meeting right now. Jake's going to be there.'

'Oh, yeah?' Gibson replied. He appeared sincere, although Curtis remained wary.

'Why don't you tag along?' Curtis asked.

'Why, that'd work fine.'

'After you put your pistol away, that is,' added Curtis pointedly.

Gibson gave a short laugh, but put his gun back in its holster.

'Not a problem, mister. You have me at a disadvantage, though. You know my name but I still don't know yours.'

'Name's Curtis. Will Curtis.' He watched Gibson's face keenly but couldn't discern any change in it after telling the man his name. His suspicions eased, but only somewhat.

Gibson pushed himself to his feet and kicked the empty bottle off into the trees. He gestured up the trail.

'Got my horse tied up about a quarter-mile thataway,' he said.

'Lead the way,' Curtis said. 'I'll bring up the rear.'

Gibson nodded and began walking up the narrow, leaf-covered path. For all the whiskey he'd consumed, he was remarkably steady on his feet. Curtis watched him closely as they moved through the dark foliage. Gibson walked with his shoulders straight and his hands loose at his sides.

'So, you from around here, Will Curtis?' Gibson asked over his shoulder.

'Nah,' said Curtis. 'From Idaho originally.'

'How'd you get mixed up in this Junction City mess?'

'Rode into town and ran into one of Clem Dawson's strongmen. He forced me to shoot him. Left a bad taste in my mouth, I guess you could say.' A crease furrowed Curtis's brow. 'How you know about what's going on in Junction City?'

'Like I said, I got kin around here,' Gibson responded easily. 'I hear things.' He pulled his coat closed against the sharp night air. 'Still, this ain't your fight. Probably caused you a lot of trouble. You ain't thought of just lighting out and looking for greener pastures?'

'Not that simple. They tried to kill my friends. They were willing to kill little kids to get what they want. I'm stickin' around until this gets resolved, one way or another.'

'Dawson tried to kill kids?' Gibson asked.

'Yeah, he did. Abe Bannerman's boys. You know old Abe, don't you?'

Ike Gibson didn't skip a beat.

'Oh, sure. I know Abe. Damn shame there are men who are willing to kill like that, just for a little money.'

Curtis was tiring of the conversation. 'Where's your horse?' he asked impatiently.

'Right up here,' said Gibson, pointing off the trail to the right.

Curtis halted his horse and looked up into the trees. He thought he could see the shape of the back end of a horse between two big maple trees up a slight rise off the trail. He rested his right hand on his thigh, poised for any surprises. He would take no chances with strangers in these parts, particularly on such an isolated trail at this time of night.

Gibson turned and grinned thinly.

'I'll just run up there and get her, if you don't mind.'

'Not a bit. Hurry up, though. I don't want to be late for that meeting.'

'Sure, sure.' Gibson started up the incline, stepping cautiously on the slippery leaves. Curtis watched him untie the horse's reins and then lead the animal back down to the trail. He could see the horse clearly in the moonlight.

'That's a damn fine mount you've got there,' Curtis said. He had always been an unabashed admirer of quality horseflesh.

Gibson patted the horse's neck. Curtis could tell the man was proud of it.

'Thanks. You wouldn't believe the offers I've gotten to sell her.' He looked into the horse's eye and spoke to her affectionately. 'Ain't that right, girl? Everybody wants to take you off my hands.' He slid his boot into a stirrup and swung up into the saddle. 'I'll tell you one thing, though. She ain't for sale. I don't know what I'd do without her.'

'A good horse is worth its weight in gold,' Curtis said, quoting one of his father's favorite expressions. 'How long have you had her?'

Gibson squinted, trying to be precise despite his whiskey-sodden state.

'Uh, it'll be three years in February. Got her in a poker game up near Seattle. Feller really didn't want to give her up, even though I won her fair and square.' He shook his head at the memory. 'We had to settle it with pistols. No way I was riding out of town on any horse but this one.' He leaned a little closer to the horse's right ear. 'Ain't that right, girl?' He patted her neck again. Curtis reckoned the man asked his horse that question a lot.

'What were you doing up in Seattle?' Curtis inquired.

'Little of this, little of that,' Gibson said. He stopped

patting the horse's neck. Curtis wondered if Gibson were tired of the conversation, too.

'All right. I'll follow you. We're going to Phil Shirreffs's place.'

Gibson's face was confused for a moment.

'I thought you said we were going to meet Jake,' he said.

'We are. Out at Phil's cabin. We always meet there before we start the patrols at night.'

'Huh,' Gibson said simply. He scratched at his ear for a moment. 'You know, I don't rightly know how to get to … Phil's place from here.'

'I thought you were from around here.'

Gibson was irritated, though he tried to hide it.

'I am from around here. Just never ridden out to Phil's from this trail. Been years since I been there.'

This was plausible to Curtis, although he remained wary.

'Well, just head straight up this trail a ways,' he said. 'The road to his ranch branches off from this one. I'll let you know when we get there.'

'OK, fine.'

Gibson neck-reined his mare and heeled her up the trail at an easy pace. Curtis followed a few horse-lengths behind. He kept his hand near the strap that tied his holster to his thigh. Gibson was clearly hammered but functioning none the less, like a true hardcore range hawk.

In his travels Curtis had known many men who could

consume enough liquor to stun your average mule. Many of these men could be in a state of extreme intoxication yet still ride a horse, win at poker, and outdraw opponents in a gunfight. Ike Gibson was that kind of man, Curtis thought. It could be dangerous to underestimate a drunkard like him.

They rode to the fork without speaking. The only sound was the smacking of their horses' hoofs on the wet ground.

As they approached the road to Shirreffs's homestead Curtis thumbed his Stetson back on his head and called to Gibson.

'Road to Phil's spread is up ahead on the right,' he said.

Gibson raised a hand in acknowledgement but said nothing. He directed his horse off the main trail onto the path to Shirreffs's cabin. Curtis maintained his cautious distance from the man ahead of him.

It was a mile before the forest started to thin around them. Curtis could see the cabin up ahead through the trees. A lantern was burning brightly in the kitchen of the house.

'It'll be good to see Phil,' said Gibson suddenly.

'Yeah? You two old friends?'

'Yep.' Gibson paused, then clarified his affirmation. 'Well, we're more like friendly acquaintances, I guess you could say.'

'I see,' Curtis said absently.

They were emerging from the trees into the large

forest pasture that was Shirreffs's yard. There was a layer of mist over the grass that obscured the hoofs of their mounts.

The trail they'd used brought them out behind the house. They rode around the corral and passed by the bunkhouse, which was in darkness. As they moved up toward the front porch Curtis was surprised to see that neither Jake Douglas nor John Wilson had tied their horses to the hitching post. They invariably arrived for the pre-patrol meeting earlier than Curtis did, in part because their homes were much closer to Phil Shirreffs's house than was the Bannermans' uncle's place.

This was the first time Curtis had arrived before Douglas or Wilson. He looked toward Ike Gibson.

'We can tie up here,' he said.

Gibson drew reins near the porch and then dismounted. Curtis followed suit seconds later. They twisted the reins around the post and Curtis put a boot on the bottom step. The front door was open slightly.

'Phil, you in there?' he said, feeling for the makings in his coat pocket. He removed the papers and the sack of tobacco and began to build a smoke in the light that shone out from the front door.

'You got an extra smoke there, partner?' asked Ike Gibson.

Despite his casual demeanour Curtis had kept a watchful eye on Gibson. The stranger hadn't made any suspicious moves.

'Sure do,' Curtis said.

He heard boots crossing the floor inside the house. The hinges groaned as the door was pulled open. Curtis looked up and his face went slack. His fingers froze in the middle of twisting the end of the cigarette.

A man stood in the doorway. In his hands was a shotgun. Both barrels were aimed at Will Curtis's head.

CHAPTER SEVEN

The man on the porch smiled, but his face was humorless.

'You go ahead and toss your pistol up here on the porch, Will Curtis,' he said.

Curtis swiveled his eyes toward Ike Gibson. He wasn't surprised to see Gibson aiming his pistol at him.

'You heard him,' Gibson said. He was smiling, too.

Curtis pulled his Navy Colt and dropped it on the edge of the porch.

'You're not as dumb as you look, Curtis,' said the man on the porch. He used the tip of his boot to bring Curtis's pistol closer. Then he bent down and picked it up. He leaned the shotgun in the doorjamb and examined the pistol. He nodded approvingly and looked back at Curtis. 'You take good care of your weapons, don't you?' he asked rhetorically. 'This looks like it was just cleaned and oiled.' He slipped the gun into his waistband.

Curtis glared at the man. 'Where's Phil Shirreffs?' he asked.

The man scoffed. 'Don't worry about Phil,' he said.

'Where're Jake Douglas and John Wilson?' Curtis demanded, undeterred.

'Like I said – don't worry. Don't worry about Phil, don't worry about Jake, don't worry about John.' The man looked at Ike Gibson. 'Tie him up, Ike.'

Gibson opened his saddlebag and removed a rope. He stepped up to Curtis, who put his hands behind his back.

'See?' Gibson said smugly. 'I like it when people cooperate. It makes things easier for everyone.'

'Shut up, you drunken ass,' Curtis said.

Both Gibson and the man on the porch laughed. Gibson pulled the knots painfully tight.

'I want to make sure your bindings are real secure,' he said with a mocking sneer.

The man on the porch gestured toward the front door.

'Bring him in, Ike,' he said.

Gibson grabbed Curtis and propelled him up the stairs and into the living room of Phil Shirreffs's home. Curtis looked around as he stepped in. There were no signs of a struggle in the room. Gibson shoved Curtis onto the couch.

'Take a load off,' he said. He leaned over and removed the tobacco and papers from Curtis's pocket. 'Never did get that cigarette.' He sank heavily into a chair across from the couch and looked at the other man, who stood near the front door, shotgun slung over the crook of his arm. 'Cobb, you got any whiskey?'

Curtis raised his head.

'Cobb?' he asked quietly. 'You're Cobb McGillicutty?'

McGillicutty was visibly annoyed. He glared at Ike Gibson for a moment before answering Curtis.

'That's right.'

'I'll be damned,' Curtis said. He let out a low whistle. 'Clem Dawson's really scraping the dregs, ain't he?'

Gibson's eyes widened and looked at McGillicutty to see how the big man would respond. McGillicutty's lips curled into a sinister grin.

'Glad to see my reputation precedes me,' he said.

Curtis was quiet, his mind racing. He knew of Cobb McGillicutty – everybody did. Everybody in the Pacific Northwest, anyway. He was a notorious gunman who was said to have killed more than a dozen men. Some of these men he'd killed because of insults or fights in saloons. Others were men he'd been hired to kill, whom he'd hunted down and executed for money.

There many lawmen in Oregon, Idaho, and Montana who wanted to hang Cobb McGillicutty. And here he was, standing casually across the room from Will Curtis. Curtis wondered how Clem Dawson had found the killer. With his connections, it probably hadn't been too hard. Curtis hadn't doubted Dawson's commitment to wiping out the homesteaders of Junction City, but he was stunned by this turn of events.

'So how about it, Cobb? You got any whiskey hiding around here?' Gibson asked.

'There's some on the table in the kitchen,' McGillicutty said. 'I found it in a cupboard.'

That was all Ike Gibson needed to hear. He strode out of the room, leaving Curtis and McGillicutty alone. Curtis decided to try to get some information from McGillicutty.

'What's all this about, Cobb?' he asked.

McGillicutty regarded him coolly.

'What do you mean?'

'I mean, why the hell does Clem Dawson want to control Junction City so bad? This is a little village out in the sticks. Dawson's already rich. What's the point of all this?'

McGillicutty picked at a cuticle for a few moments.

'I guess it don't make much difference if you know or not,' he said. Curtis understood his meaning. It didn't make a difference what Curtis knew because Curtis would soon be dead. 'You see, Mr Dawson has big plans. He's going to build a railway station right here in Junction City.'

Curtis was incredulous.

'That's worth killing people over?'

McGillicutty shrugged.

'To Clem Dawson it is. And he pays good money to get what he wants.'

They were interrupted by Gibson, who walked back into the living room with a half-empty whiskey bottle in his hand. He stopped and took a giant swig, then wiped his sleeve across his lips.

'That's good stuff!' he proclaimed. He stepped back to his chair and was sitting down when the sound of approaching horses brought him back to a standing position. 'That must be them,' he said to McGillicutty.

'Bring him out,' McGillicutty commanded. He turned and walked out onto the porch to meet the approaching horsemen.

Gibson grabbed Curtis and yanked him roughly to his feet.

'Come out and say hello to your pards,' he said. He pushed Curtis forward and they joined McGillicutty on the porch.

There were six men on horses. As the riders got closer to the porch and the light shining from within the cabin, Curtis recognized Jake Douglas and John Wilson in the front of the pack. Their faces were swollen, bloody, and bruised, and their hands were tied together in front of them. The group stopped a few feet from the front steps. Gibson and McGillicutty walked down and helped pull Douglas and Wilson from the saddles. They let the two men fall into the dirt beside their horses.

Curtis scanned the faces of the other four riders, but none was familiar. Clearly these were more of Dawson's hired enforcers. The men dismounted and tied their horses to the hitching post.

Douglas and Wilson struggled up to sitting positions, spitting dirt and stray blades of grass from their mouths. Douglas's beating had obviously been particularly brutal: probably, Curtis thought, because of the man's massive size. He was more of a threat than small John Wilson was, although Wilson was a fighter, too.

Jake Douglas looked at Curtis through swollen eyes.

'Howdy, Will,' he said.

'Damn, Jake,' Curtis said with concern. 'They really put you through the wringer, didn't they?'

Douglas coughed wretchedly and a stream of blood poured from his mouth. He leaned forward and let it drip into the dirt.

'Yeah, they're pretty tough,' he said. 'Well, when you get all four of them together. I don't think any of them wanted to tangle one on one.'

The look in Jake Douglas's eyes was savage and bloodthirsty. The four gunmen responded with a show of bravado, partly to save face in front of Cobb McGillicutty.

'Now don't go flattering yourself, Douglas,' one of the men said. 'You can't win 'em all.' The man raised a muddy boot and kicked Douglas hard in the side of his head, sending him toppling back onto his side with a groan.

McGillicutty observed this interaction without apparent interest.

'All right,' he said. 'Let's finish this job up.' He glanced at Ike Gibson and nodded.

'What're you doing?' Curtis asked, his pulse roaring in his ears.

'Watch and you'll see,' Gibson said with a snicker.

He stepped off the porch and the four other Dawson men stepped away, leaving a clear space around Douglas and Wilson. Gibson grabbed John Wilson's hair and yanked the man to his feet.

'Git up, you!' he snarled. Wilson struggled to maintain his balance and finally succeeded. Gibson turned and addressed himself to Will Curtis, who stood watching with his jaw set in a grim line. 'This,' Gibson continued, 'is what happens when you cross the wrong people in Junction City.'

Without further ado, he pulled his pistol from his holster, placed it up against Wilson's forehead, and fired. Blood spurted from the rancher's head and his body collapsed onto the ground.

'No!' yelled Curtis. He took a step forward but halted when Cobb McGillicutty gripped his shoulder. 'You sidewinding bastards,' he cursed. 'You just killed a good man.'

The gunmen laughed, some uproariously. Two of them lifted Jake Douglas by his shoulders and pushed him forward toward Gibson. Douglas's bloody face was resigned. He almost hadn't had time to begin despairing.

Gibson raised his pistol and pressed it up against Douglas's temple. Gibson pulled the trigger and Douglas's body joined that of Wilson in the dirt with a sickening thud. Blood poured from the side of his head. Gibson had a satisfied smile on his face as he slid the pistol back into the holster.

Curtis's body tensed and his wrists pulled against his bindings.

'You're going to pay for that, Gibson,' he said, his lips pulled tight against his teeth.

'Who's going to make me pay?' Gibson asked. 'You?'

'Why don't you take these bindings off and we can answer that right here. Man to man.'

Gibson laughed disdainfully. 'Yeah, sure,' he said.

When his fellow gunmen looked at him questioningly nervousness manifested itself in a strange twitch in Gibson's right eye.

'Y'all heard what Dawson said. He wants us to bring in Curtis in good shape. I wouldn't want to spoil his pretty looks.'

'Just like I thought,' Curtis said. 'A coward to the core.'

Ike Gibson was dangerously close to losing face in front of his peers. He decided he had to act. He stepped toward Curtis and grabbed the front of his shirt. He lifted his hand and brought it hard across Curtis's face in a dismissive, insulting slap. Curtis's head barely moved, and his angry stare remained locked on Gibson's face.

'Let's get outta here,' Gibson said angrily, as if he could recover his dignity by barking commands.

He turned and took a step toward the hitching post. With blinding speed Curtis struck out with his right foot, catching Gibson in the shins. Gibson's feet flew out from under him and he smashed face first into the hard dirt. The impact was powerful, and some of Gibson's colleagues stifled laughs.

'How'd that taste?' Curtis asked.

Dazed and still quite drunk, Ike Gibson stood up slowly and a little uncertainly. His rheumy eyes darted around the circle of men in the yard, then his hand went for the pistol on his hip.

'That's enough!' Cobb McGillicutty hollered. All heads turned to him. His shotgun was back in his hands, aimed at Gibson.

'What the hell are you doing?' Gibson asked hoarsely. He had a deep gash on his chin and two of his front teeth were bloodied and dangling from his gums at an awkward angle.

'We're getting paid to do a job, you pathetic drunk,' said McGillicutty. 'You get your hand off that gun. Curtis has an appointment in Junction City.'

Gibson's hands dangled once more at his sides. He was careful to keep them well away from his gun.

'Now y'all get back on your horses. Help Curtis onto his. We're running late.'

The men obeyed instantly. McGillicutty selected two of the men to stay at Shirreffs's cabin.

'Tomorrow there'll be homesteader scum coming 'round to see where the patrollers are and why they ain't come home. Close the shutters and be ready for them. You know the plan, so I shouldn't have to explain it again.' He paused and looked hard at the two who were staying behind. 'Right?'

'Oh, right, Cobb,' said one of the men eagerly. 'We know what we're doing.'

'Yeah, well, sometimes I wonder,' McGillicutty said, his words clearly directed at Ike Gibson. He descended from the porch and climbed up onto his horse. 'Let's get out of here.'

The men rode across the yard into the forest, with Will Curtis directly in front of Cobb McGillicutty.

A cold drizzle began to fall as the forest swallowed them. Ike Gibson, riding just ahead of Curtis, occasionally looked over his shoulder and shot a hateful glance at the man who'd humiliated him so badly. Gibson's entire livelihood depended on his reputation for toughness and action. To be kicked into the dirt by what the other gunmen considered a two-bit ranch hand was bad enough. To be kicked in the dirt by a two-bit ranch hand whose hands were tied behind his back was thoroughly beyond the pale for a man such as Gibson.

Curtis ignored him, his mind focusing on the changing situation that now faced the people of the Junction City hill country.

Jake Douglas and John Wilson, two of the most reliable and courageous of the local ranchers, were dead, shot by a hired assassin while tied up and unarmed. Phil Shirreffs was missing and Curtis presumed he was dead. Curtis had been captured and was being taken into town. He had no doubt that Clem Dawson had special plans for him. The banker's desire for vengeance after the earlier encounter with Curtis had overtaken virtually all other concerns in his life.

Mostly, though, Curtis thought of the Bannermans.

Dawson now had a foothold in the hills from which to operate against his enemies. It was only a matter of time before the man struck, and now he had the element of surprise on his side.

CHAPTER EIGHT

Clem Dawson smoothed out his silk tie and flicked some stray cigar ash from his lapel. Then he looked across his desk at the man sitting opposite him and smiled unctuously.

'You really have gone above and beyond the call of duty,' he said, his voice smooth and confident.

'I didn't really have any other choice,' the other man said grimly.

'True,' Dawson said with a sly chuckle.

'I don't know why that's so funny.'

The smile faded slowly from Clem Dawson's lips. His eyes were like black, bottomless pools.

'I'm a business man,' he said. 'Sometimes I have to make decisions that others might find ... unsavory. I have come to accept this as the price I pay for my success. Ultimately I think I've been more than generous with you, all things considered.'

'Yeah? How you figure?'

'I could have simply thrown you out of your home

with no kind of compensation. That would have been well within my legal rights as the holder of your mortgage.' He settled back in his chair and drew deeply on his fragrant cigar. 'Instead, I have compensated you handsomely.'

'Well, you got what you wanted in return, too. Don't forget that.'

Dawson nodded. 'Yes, the information you gave us was vital to turning the tables on your neighbors.'

'We'll see about that.'

'Oh, we will.' Dawson's eyes were slitted. 'And you'd better hope things go my way. I could make things very awkward for you.'

'We had a deal.'

'We did. As of right now, we still do.'

'You got what you wanted. I showed your boys where all the secret trails are. I told you when we were meeting and who would be there. Without that, you'd never have found a way to spring a trap.'

'Indeed. I'm not arguing about that.' He rubbed his eyes for a moment. The entire exchange had become distasteful and he wanted the man out of his office. 'You've received your payment?'

'Yeah.'

'Good. Did you count it?'

'Yeah, I counted it.'

'All there?'

'Yeah.'

'Good. Now get the hell out of my office and don't

ever come back.'

'I couldn't come back here even if I wanted to.'

'You're right,' Dawson said. He examined the tip of his cigar as if it were a fascinating artefact. 'The name of Phil Shirreffs will be mud in Junction City for at least the next fifty years.'

Shirreffs's face reflected the impotent anger that welled within him. Without another word he turned and strode out of Clem Dawson's office, slamming the door behind him.

His horse was waiting for him in Dawson's back yard, where it was roped to a tree. He mounted and entered the alley behind the house, passing one of the guards who lurked in the shadows there. The man gave him no greeting, and Shirreffs didn't acknowledge him.

I had no other choice, he thought. *I could either lose everything and have nothing to show for all the years of hard work, or I could take Dawson's offer and have a chance to make a new life somewhere else. Besides, it was inevitable that Dawson would win in the end. He had all the advantages, and his men were committed to Dawson's cause. His money made sure of that.*

Shirreffs leaned over and spat tobacco juice into the bushes that grew along the left side of the alley.

He had had this same internal discussion with himself countless times in the two weeks since he'd received the formal legal letter telling him he was about to lose his home and property. Along with the letter was a personal note from Clem Dawson.

Dawson had read his man well, Shirreffs thought with intense self-disgust.

He was out of town heading south within a few minutes of leaving Dawson's yard. He figured he'd just keep on heading south, out of Oregon. He'd spend a little time in California, then maybe continue on to Mexico. He'd heard good things about Mexico. The gold coins to the tune of $1,000 that he'd received from Dawson would go a long way, south of the border.

He'd only made it three miles out of town when the two riders emerged from the trees, one ahead of Shirreffs and one behind him. Shirreffs pulled reins, his heart pounding. In an instant he was soaked in sweat.

'Evening, Phil,' said the man in front of him. 'Nice night for a ride, don't you think?'

'What the hell do you want?' Shirreffs asked.

He wasn't a cowardly man, but his chest was filled with a stark terror he'd never before experienced.

'Mr Dawson was doing some thinking,' the man behind Shirreffs said. The rancher hipped in the saddle and squinted toward him. 'He thinks he overpaid you.'

'I was just in his office and he didn't say anything like that!'

'He probably didn't want to make a scene,' said the man in front.

'Yeah,' said the man in back. 'Mr Dawson just hates scenes.'

Both gunmen snickered.

'We had a deal,' Shirreffs said. 'Get out of my way

and let me go.'

'Afraid we can't do that, Phil.'

There was no alternative. Shirreffs recognized this now. In desperation, his hand reached for the rifle in the scabbard beside him.

The two gunmen were thorough professionals. They sank six bullets into Phil Shirreffs's chest and back before he'd even got a firm grip on the butt of his rifle. He fell out of the saddle onto the cold ground and didn't move.

The gunmen dismounted and dragged his body deep into the thick brush beside the trail. One of the men opened one of Shirreffs's saddlebags and removed a bulky bag of coins from it. Then he slapped the horse on the rump and the animal broke into a gallop, heading south on the road toward Eugene.

The two men clambered up onto their mounts and rode back to Junction City.

Clem Dawson looked at the massive clock on the wall of his office. It was just after two o'clock in the morning. If everything had gone according to plan, he would soon be expected at the barn on the edge of town. He stabbed his cigar out in the ornate ashtray and rose. There was a bar set into the wall across the room and Dawson poured himself a stiff brandy. He finished it in two quick gulps and stepped out into the hallway.

The house was in silence. He listened for any sounds from Alvin's room upstairs, but there were none.

Dawson left through the back door. The guard was waiting for him there. Dawson retrieved his horse from the stable and the guard untied his mount from a pole near the fence.

Junction City was like a ghost town as they rode through its streets. On the north-western outskirts of the town, set a few dozen yards back from the street, was a large barn. Dawson kept several horses, a wagon, and two buggies there. Unless Dawson were going to Eugene or Salem, the barn was virtually never used.

Tonight, however, lanterns were burning in the wide aisle between the stalls. Two more guards met Dawson at the back entrance to the barn. He dismounted and entered the building. He saw that the mission had been a success and he was filled with a feeling of deep pleasure.

Will Curtis was tied to a chair in the center of the aisle. He was stripped to the waist and Dawson saw that his orders to the guards had been obeyed. Curtis hadn't been beaten or abused.

A door opened near Dawson and Cobb McGillicutty stepped out of the store room. He closed the door behind him and nodded toward Dawson.

'You did good work,' Dawson said. He reached into his breast pocket and pulled out a cheroot. 'Now I want all of you out of here. Wait outside and keep a good eye out. I'll call you when I need you.'

'Yes, sir,' said McGillicutty. He motioned to the two guards standing near the rear stalls and they followed him out into the yard behind the barn.

Dawson stepped out of the shadows and walked toward Curtis. He stopped a few feet away and struck a match on one of the stall doors. He lighted the cheroot and stared at Curtis through the smoke.

'Good to see you again, Dawson,' Curtis said sarcastically. His face was defiant as he glared at the banker.

'Yeah, I'm sure,' Dawson retorted with a smile. His right hand was still in a bandage from the bullet wound he'd received from Curtis that night in Dawson's bedroom. He looked at the bandage absently.

'How's that hand treating you?' Curtis asked.

Dawson's eyes glinted as he chewed on the cheroot.

'You got a real smart mouth on you, Curtis.'

'That's what people tell me.'

'Hmmm. I think after tonight you just might learn to tame that sharp tongue of yours.'

'You think so?'

'I do. I think you're going to be a different man in a few hours.'

Curtis glanced toward the door where the guards had exited.

'I guess you better call in your boys, Clem.'

'Don't worry – I'll call them in when it's time.'

Smoke billowed out of Dawson's flared nostrils and Curtis regarded him curiously.

'What are you waiting for?' he asked.

'I just wanted to get a good look at the man who's caused all this trouble for me. You're not even from around these parts. What's your game?'

'I ain't got any game.'

'There must be some reason you've chosen to insert yourself in my affairs.'

'All this business that's been going on ain't just your affair, Clem.' Curtis spat contemptuously into the dirt near Dawson's feet, narrowly missing the man's polished shoes. Dawson stepped a little further back from Curtis.

'How do you figure?' Dawson asked.

'You can't just force people off their own land, or bully people into giving you whatever you want.'

'I made all those people very generous offers.'

'Sure you did. And if they chose not to accept, then you tried to burn them and their children alive.'

'As I told you before, that had nothing to do with me.'

'Spare me your bullshit. I ain't buying it.'

'Fair enough,' said Dawson.

He rolled the cheroot from one side of his mouth to the other as he regarded Curtis. The latter was puzzled by Dawson's desire to converse, particularly since it was plain as day that Dawson intended to have Curtis killed.

Why is he taking the time to have this little chat? Curtis wondered. The entire exchange was bizarre.

'Since you're in a mood to talk, why don't you tell me what your big plans are for Junction City? I asked your boy McGillicutty, but he ain't really the explaining type, if you know what I'm saying.'

'My plans for Junction City?' Dawson asked

innocently.

'Yeah. Whatever scheme you've got up your sleeve, it must be pretty big to justify killing so many people.'

'Like I said, that was an unfortunate—'

'You want to tell that to the families of Jake Douglas and John Wilson?'

Dawson shrugged. 'Those gentlemen had their chance to make the right decision ...'

'And where the hell is Phil Shirreffs?'

'Mr Shirreffs? Last I heard he'd taken leave of Junction City. Headed south somewhere, from what I understand.'

'I don't believe you,' Curtis said. 'I'm sure he's dead, just like anyone around here who has the audacity to defy you. But go ahead – tell me about how you plan on building Rome in a day.'

Dawson looked down at the dirt floor. He moved some hay around with the tip of his shoe.

'I guess I might as well tell you,' he said. 'After all, you're going to be dead in a few hours, so you won't be able to throw a wrench in the works anyway.'

'Don't worry, Clem. I won't share any of your precious secrets.'

Dawson grinned. 'You know, you are amusing in many respects, Will Curtis. It's a shame you picked the wrong side in this fight.'

'I didn't have much choice. Your moron son made it for me.'

'Ah, yes,' Dawson said with a sigh. 'Alvin. He's never

really been the same since his mother died.'

'Poor kid. I'm sure he's got a heart of gold.'

This time Dawson laughed out loud.

'No, not Alvin. He's too much like me.' He pulled his watch out of one of his breast pockets and checked the time. 'You wanted to know why I have such an interest in controlling Junction City. Well, I'll tell you now, and then our business will be completed. Junction City has the potential to be a major center for the cattle business. I intend to buy up all the land in the area and import cattle. Thousands of Herefords, shipped here directly from Texas. This kind of undertaking needs centralization and someone who knows how to, shall we say, manipulate the levers of power in order to get things done.'

Curtis watched Dawson carefully as the latter spoke. A thin sheen of sweat lay over the man's features. His eyes sparkled with enthusiasm as he detailed his ambitions.

'I must say, when I made my offers to the local ranchers and homesteaders, I figured they would recognize my generosity and be reasonable. The only way I can operate on the scale I have in mind is by getting the rights to the land and water around this town. As you know, this is a very fertile area, with almost unlimited resources. Why, I reckon I could recoup all of my investment in the first year after the cattle arrive. By the end of the second year, I guarantee I could bring in between two- and three-hundred thousand dollars. And that's just the beginning.'

'These hundreds of thousands of dollars – they going to benefit you or the entire town?' Curtis asked.

There was a hint of disappointment in Dawson's face as he answered Curtis's question, as if he had suddenly realized he was speaking to an idiot.

'I don't think you understand, Curtis. What's good for me is good for Junction City. I'm going to put this little podunk town on the map.' His chest puffed as he spoke. 'I'd say that's more than the people around here deserve.'

'There's one thing you seem to have forgotten while you were making all these plans, Dawson.'

'What's that?'

'How are you going to get all the cattle here?'

Dawson waved a hand dismissively.

'That's all taken care of,' he explained. 'We're going to build a railroad depot right here in Junction City. I have lots of friends in the railroad industry, you see. We're going to build cattle pens on a grand scale. That, too, will be a benefit to the ... local economy. Once we get the railway established here and bring in the cows from Texas, well – there's really no limit to what can be accomplished. A few hundred thousand dollars is only the beginning, you see.'

He removed another cheroot from his pocket and lighted it with the tip of his last one. 'In ten years, the cattle industry here will be worth well over a million dollars per year.' His eyes sparkled with expectant triumph. 'Just imagine that, Curtis. The profits will only increase, and they'll do so every year. And I will be the biggest cattle baron north of California.'

'You sound like Napoleon,' Curtis said. 'Your brain must be fuzzier than a grizzly's ass.'

The humor left Clem Dawson's face.

'We'll see about that, Curtis,' he said. 'Or, at least, some of us will see about that.'

In a swift movement that caught Curtis by surprise, Dawson stepped forward and grabbed Curtis's hair, yanking his head to the side. He thrust the fiery tip of his cheroot into the side of Curtis's neck and twisted it. Curtis howled as the scent of his own burning flesh filled his nostrils. Then Dawson stepped back, flicking the remainder of the small cigar into the seated man's face.

'You son of a bitch,' Curtis said, wincing from the searing pain of the burn.

'That's just the beginning,' Dawson declared. He buttoned his coat neatly and smoothed his hair. 'There's someone who wants to see you. An old friend, you could say.' He turned and looked toward the store room door from which Cobb McGillicutty had emerged several minutes before. Lantern light showed in the crack near the floor. 'You can come on out,' he said loudly, and then turned back to Curtis.

The door opened and a small figure emerged, his body supported on the right by a crutch. Curtis couldn't make out who it was in the darkness near the back door.

'I think you remember Mr Mack Kantor, don't you, Curtis?' Dawson asked. 'He's been recuperating at a hospital in Eugene since last you met, but he jumped at the chance to renew your acquaintance.'

CHAPTER NINE

Mack Kantor moved slowly out of the shadows at the back of the barn, his crutch scraping in the dirt as he moved forward. It was only when he was about fifteen feet from Curtis that the latter saw the extent of Kantor's injury.

His right foot had been amputated right above the ankle where Curtis had shot him. A thick cloth bandage had been wrapped repeatedly around the lower part of his leg. He hobbled until he was a few feet away from Clem Dawson and then stopped, staring at Will Curtis with an oblique glance. The fingers on Kantor's left hand were splayed out in an awkward fashion where Curtis had stepped on them at the cabin.

'Well, would you look at that,' Kantor said. 'How the mighty have fallen.'

Curtis was still a little woozy from the cigar burn on his neck. He had to concentrate extra hard in order to insult the crippled bushwhacker who stood before him.

'Boy, that's quite a job the doctor did,' he rasped. 'I

guess you won't be winning any three-legged races any time soon, huh, Mack?'

'You smart-mouthed bastard,' said Kantor, his face contorted with loathing and a desire for vengeance. 'Keep flapping those gums. You won't be laughing for much longer, I promise you that.'

'I seem to recall you specialize in killing old men, Mack. I guess you also like it when the men you torture are tied to a chair, is that right?'

Kantor ignored Curtis's taunts and shifted his beady eyes to Clem Dawson.

'You all set, boss?'

'I'm finished with him,' Dawson affirmed.

'Good.'

'You have about four hours, Mack. I trust you can find some way to amuse yourself at Mr Curtis's expense.'

'Don't you worry, Mr Dawson,' Kantor said, looking again at Will Curtis. 'This is going to be a night that neither of us will ever forget.'

'Fine, then. I'll be off.' Dawson slipped his derby hat back on his head and grinned at the prisoner. 'Do try to die like a man, Will Curtis. I would be disappointed if you did otherwise.'

With that, Clem Dawson pivoted and left the barn through the back door, leaving Curtis and Kantor alone.

Kantor limped closer to his prey.

'My goodness, that is one nasty burn on your neck. Yes, indeedy. Must've hurt like hell, am I right?' he said with a laugh.

'Probably didn't hurt half as much when I shot you in the ankle. You were really running that time. Guess you ain't doing much running these days.'

'Shut up,' said Kantor.

He backhanded Curtis across the face viciously, then dug his thumbnail deep into the burn on the man's neck. Curtis yelled with pain, and a smile of pleasure crossed Mack Kantor's face.

'Yes, yes – that's more like it,' Kantor intoned. His voice was oddly clinical as he began his work. 'You don't know how long I've been waiting to see you again, Will.' He used the crutch to move back a couple of feet and then, balancing on his left foot, he drove the end of the crutch into Curtis's throat.

Curtis gagged and then vomited on himself. His eyes welled from the pain as he struggled to catch his breath.

'Mm-hmm,' Kantor said. 'Been thinking about this little reunion of ours for months now. I had nothing better to do, sitting around in that hospital in Eugene. Every day I thought about you.'

'I'm flattered,' Curtis said.

'You should be. I've wanted to hurt people before in my life, there's no doubt about that. And I have killed a lot of people. But there ain't never been nobody I wanted to hurt like I want to hurt you.'

Curtis's arms were tied securely behind him, so that he was no threat to his tormentor. Kantor leaned in and punched him as hard as he could across the bridge of the nose. Bright lights exploded in Curtis's eyes as blood burst from his nose and streamed down his face, dripping off his chin onto his shirt.

'How you like that?' Kantor asked.

Curtis, barely conscious, didn't respond. Kantor brought his arm back and punched Curtis again, this time flattening his nose grotesquely. More blood flowed onto Curtis's shirt. His head drooped forward and the blood flowed onto his pants and then onto the dirt floor.

'Damn, you're bleeding like a stuck pig, Curtis!' Kantor exclaimed. There was exuberance in his voice. 'You're going to need to get the doc to check out that nose. It ain't looking so good.' He giggled at his own cleverness, and his power.

Curtis's brain reeled and he struggled to stay conscious. He blinked a few times. He could see Kantor's foot and the crutch on the ground before him. Pain assailed him, from his nose, his throat, and the burn on his neck.

'Thaaaaat's right,' Kantor said, almost soothingly. 'It hurts, don't it? Pain like that can take some getting used to.'

Curtis tried to raise his head to face his tormentor but failed. He heard a low moan of agony. It took a few moments for him to register that he was the one making the noise.

'You know, I thought I understood what pain was until you shot me in the foot. That's when I learned a whole new lesson about pain. Yes, sir, I did. They took me into Eugene and dumped me at the sawbones' place. I mean it, too – they just dumped me right in his goddamn yard in the rain, middle of the night and everything.'

Curtis realized that Kantor was talking to himself as much as he was to his prisoner.

'I told the doc I'd kill him if he cut my foot off. I said I'd rather die than lose my damn foot.'

Through his hazy vision, Curtis saw something glinting in the lantern light. He couldn't tell what it was, but suddenly it moved from the right side of his line of sight to the left, then back again.

Still Mack Kantor droned on.

'Wouldn't you know, the varmint did it anyway. He cut my foot off! When I woke up he said if he hadn't cut it off an infection would've set in and killed me.'

The mysterious shiny object moved again.

'Thing is, I'm glad he did it now. Gave me the chance to come back to Junction City and spend a little time with my old friend, Will Curtis.'

Kantor emitted a maniacal laugh and the shiny object moved swiftly toward Curtis. He felt a hot, sudden pain on the side of his face, and then he was aware of more blood flowing, this time down his face and onto his neck and shoulder. The pain intensified and he realized he'd been cut, and pretty deeply, too.

It was a knife he'd seen moving in Kantor's hands. A very sharp knife.

His mind began to clear and, just as it did so, Kantor

made another move toward Curtis, who felt a sharp pain along the upper left side of his chest, cutting through his shirt to pierce the flesh. Then the tip of the blade gouged into his collarbone, sinking through the flesh and gouging the bone itself. The mostly healed bullet wound in his ribcage began to throb for the first time in weeks. Curtis's vision cleared and he screamed in pain.

Kantor's smiled widened and he withdrew the blade. Curtis felt a few seconds of relief, but Kantor wasn't done. He drove the blade again into the wound he'd just made, harder this time. Again Curtis screamed, and again Kantor laughed.

Kantor removed the knife and took a deep breath.

'That feels good, don't it?' he asked.

He slipped the knife into his waistband. Again he balanced on his one good foot and struck Curtis with the crutch, this time in the mouth rather than in the nose. Curtis's head whiplashed back, spewing blood. His lips split and began to swell almost immediately.

Kantor was gleeful.

'Goddamn!' he exulted. 'You sure know how to bleed.'

He hit Curtis with the crutch, again in the mouth.

'You got anything to say, cowboy?' he taunted.

'Yeah,' Curtis said.

'Speak up.'

'Yeah … I got something to say.'

Kantor leaned forward slightly.

'Spit it out.'

'I wanted to tell you that ... that ... I never did meet a more sorry, lily-livered sack of shit in my entire life than Mack Kantor.'

Kantor's good humor evaporated instantly. He lifted the crutch again and smashed it with all his strength into Curtis's face. This time the chair tumbled over backward and Curtis crashed to the floor with immense force. The wind was knocked out of him and his hands were pinned beneath him. He wheezed and coughed, turning his head to the side to allow the blood from his mouth and nose to pour onto the ground rather than down his gullet. Hideous gurgling noises escaped from his throat.

'That's what your smart mouth will get you,' Kantor hissed. 'And there's a lot more where that came from. You better believe it.'

Kantor was interrupted when someone opened the back door of the barn and spoke to him.

'Hey, Mack—'

'You dumb bastard! I said nobody better interrupt me.'

'I know, but you also said you wanted some whiskey. Well, we just got our hands on a bottle.'

Kantor's tone softened.

'All right, then. Bring it in.'

The man shook his head.

'Can't do that, Mack. We're passing it around. If you want some, you'll have to come and get your share.'

Kantor considered the offer.

'Fine. I'll come out,' he said. He looked down at Curtis. 'Don't go anywhere, y'hear? We ain't finished yet.'

Curtis said nothing. He could hear Kantor's crutch scraping through the dirt and then the back door of the barn slammed shut.

Instantly Curtis was in motion. He shifted his body weight with as much momentum as he could muster and the chair fell onto its side. When Kantor had knocked Curtis over he'd inadvertently broken the back of the chair. Curtis pushed against the ropes around his wrists and the back of the chair broke off cleanly from the seat, releasing the ropes from where they'd been tied to the chair.

Working frantically, he was able to loosen the ropes from his wrists, aided in part by the sweat that covered his entire body. Once his hands were free he began to work on the ropes around his ankles.

He could hear the men talking and laughing loudly outside, their high spirits lubricated by the jug of whiskey they were sharing. Curtis fought back a powerful urge to panic and kept his mind focused intently on untying the ropes at his feet. It took less than a minute to get his legs free, but it felt like an eternity, so acutely conscious was he of Kantor's imminent return.

Once his legs were free he got an unexpected burst of energy. He was working now purely on adrenaline and fear, driven by the will to survive. Barely conscious of his own movements, he found himself on his feet, moving toward the back of the barn where the store room door stood ajar.

He had nearly reached the store room when the back door of the barn opened.

CHAPTER TEN

It was two hours after dawn and the homesteaders had Phil Shirreffs's cabin surrounded.

Sally Bannerman lay in some brush between two large maple trees, her father's pistol in hand and a Winchester rifle in the grass nearby. Abe Bannerman bellied up beside her.

'Is everybody here?' she asked.

'Yep,' her brother said. He gestured at various points in the trees around the cabin. 'Mike Tancred's there, Gil Harmon's over there, and Dean Taggart's covering the back door.'

The bodies of Jake Douglas and John Wilson were still in the yard where Dawson's men had left them the night before. Both of the Bannerman siblings tried to avert their eyes from the corpses of their longtime friends and neighbors, but they weren't able to do so and continue to keep a watch on the front of the cabin at the same time.

It was a little after dawn when Abe Bannerman had

ridden out to the Shirreffs property to see where Will Curtis was. He'd made it to within ten yards of the cabin when the shooting began. The men inside were so drunk they hadn't heard him approach. The liquor also affected their aim, and he escaped intact, although his favorite horse had a deep bullet burn across its chest.

There was no question now that Clem Dawson was making his move against the country dwellers around Junction City. Bannerman had alerted Tancred, Harmon, and Taggart, and now they were ready for anything Dawson's men had to offer.

Sally had insisted on joining them, and her brother had known better than to argue. He had no credible argument to make, since Sally was an excellent shot with both pistols and rifles. He could have tried to argue that women had no place taking part in gunplay, but that wouldn't have gotten far with his sister.

'I wonder where Will is,' she said. 'Phil, too.'

'They killed Jake and John right here in the yard,' her brother responded somberly. 'Didn't even bother to bury them.' He shook his head with disgust. 'You don't get much lower than that.'

'And their hands are still tied behind them.'

'Never seen anything like it in my life. Not to mention having to look at Pa's grave every day. Can't believe this is what things have come to in Junction City.'

Bannerman looked past the bodies and cupped his hands on both sides of his mouth.

'You in there,' he yelled. 'You're surrounded. There's

no way for you to escape. Come on out and surrender.'

A voice bellowed from inside the cabin. 'Why don't you come on in and get us, Bannerman!'

'You really want to die for Clem Dawson?' Bannerman replied. 'You think that rich bastard gives a damn about you?'

A second voice responded from inside, somewhere near the front door as far as Sally Bannerman could tell.

'What are you going to do if we come out?'

'We'll just have ourselves a little talk.'

'Uh huh. Then what? You'll have yourselves a little hanging?'

'We'll turn you over to the law in Eugene.'

'We are the law.' It was the first voice again. 'We're deputy sheriffs, in case you forgot.'

'I've never heard of deputy sheriffs executing unarmed men with their hands tied behind their backs,' said Bannerman angrily. 'But we won't be taking the law into our own hands. We'll turn you over to the sheriff himself, just like I said.'

There was a pause.

'We had nothing to do with shooting those two out in the yard.'

'Of course you didn't.' Bannerman's voice was thick with suspicion.

'All right, then – what was it y'all are wanting to talk about?'

'We want to know where Will Curtis and Phil Shirreffs are.'

'We don't know.'

'What d'you mean, you don't know? This is Phil's spread. I'm sure he didn't just invite you in.'

'See, that's where you're wrong, Bannerman. Phil Shirreffs is working for Clem Dawson now.'

The blood drained from Abe Bannerman's face. He and Sally exchanged glances.

'I don't believe you,' he yelled.

'It's the truth. If it weren't, his body'd be laying out there in the dirt with those other two.'

'Where's Will Curtis, then?' Sally interjected.

'We don't know. Dawson took him into town.'

'Where?'

'Don't know. Cobb said something earlier about some barn on the north edge of town.'

'Cobb?' called Abe Bannerman urgently. 'You mean Cobb McGillicutty?'

'That's the one.'

'He's working for Dawson, too?'

'That he is.'

Abe and Sally Bannerman conferred quietly before he resumed the discussion with the gunmen.

'Come on out. You got no other choice. Like we said, we'll treat you fairly and take you into Eugene, let the sheriff sort it out.'

'No tricks?'

'No tricks. You have my word.'

Nearly a minute went by as the two men inside considered their options. Finally they recognized the futility of staying inside the cabin.

'All right,' said the second man. 'We're coming out. We want to go to Eugene right away, y'hear?'

'Fine,' called Bannerman, who had no intention of carrying out their request immediately.

The people surrounding the cabin could hear the plank being raised from behind the front door. Then the door opened slowly and a man appeared in the doorway.

'Coming out now,' he said.

He stepped out onto the porch and began to descend the steps.

'Where's your pard?' Abe Bannerman demanded.

'He's coming,' said the gunman.

'Get your hands up, you,' called Mike Tancred from his position across the yard.

The man halted uncertainly and started to raise his arms. Then he made his choice and drew his pistol. He raised it and began to fire toward Tancred.

'Get down!' Bannerman commanded his sister.

The words had scarcely left his mouth when the other gunman burst out of the cabin, two six-guns drawn. The men made for their horses at the hitching post. Mike Tancred fired at the first man, who doubled over for a moment, clutching his stomach. He raised his gun and fired again toward Tancred, but his shot was wild.

Tancred took careful aim and hit the man in the head. His body fell into the dirt only a few feet away from the body of Jake Douglas.

Desperate, aware of the futility of trying to shoot it out but also aware of the noose that likely awaited him if he surrendered, the other gunman turned to where the Bannermans were crouching in the trees. Pistols blazing, his aim was surprisingly accurate. Leaves and branches burst over the Bannermans' heads.

'I've got this,' Sally Bannerman said thinly.

She lifted the pistol and fired once. The man in the yard took a bullet directly to the heart. His arms fell to his side and his pistols fell from his fingers. He took a step backward, trying to keep his balance, then fell dead onto the steps of Phil Shirreffs's cabin.

Abe Bannerman let out a low whistle.

'By God, Sally,' he said. 'That was a damn fine shot.'

Sally lowered the pistol and smiled wanly.

'He earned it,' she said, her cheeks flushed.

Tancred, Harmon, and Taggart stepped out from the trees and began walking toward the bodies that now littered the front yard. Abe Bannerman stood up and helped his sister to her feet. He put out a hand and she gave him her father's pistol. She retrieved the Winchester from the ground and handed that to him as well.

'We're going to get a few more of our neighbors,' Bannerman said. 'Then we're going into Junction City to finish this.'

'That's some good stuff right there,' said Mack Kantor.

He was still facing outward, talking to the other men outside, as he backed awkwardly through the back door of the barn, pushing it open with his shoulder.

Curtis had taken cover against the wall. As Kantor opened the door, Curtis was hidden behind it. He held his breath, keenly aware that one word from Kantor would alert Dawson's men in the yard outside.

Kantor turned around and was still mumbling approvingly to himself as he looked down the aisle between the stalls. His eyes widened in alarm and he opened his mouth to speak.

'What the—?'

Curtis slipped in behind him, shutting the door as he did so. His mind was remarkably clear now. Kantor turned his head and Curtis could smell the fresh whiskey fumes coming off the man. He clamped his left hand hard over Kantor's mouth and reached into the killer's waistband with his right hand. He pulled Kantor's knife out and drove it firmly into the side of his neck.

The crutch dropped away and thudded onto the floor. Kantor's body stiffened briefly, then went completely limp in Curtis's arms. Blood spurted across Curtis's sleeve and down his arm.

The entire exchange had taken less than fifteen seconds.

He dragged Kantor's body into an empty stall and dumped it onto a pile of hay. Then he went into the store room to look for weapons.

The room contained mostly livery supplies, with some barrels stacked against the wall. Kantor's gunbelt lay over the back of a chair near a rolltop desk in the corner.

Curtis strapped it on, then removed the pistol and checked the cartridges. Satisfied, he wiped the blood off the blade of Kantor's knife with a rag from the desk. He put the knife in his belt and stepped back into the barn.

He could hear the voices of the gunmen outside. There was no indication that the men had heard Curtis kill Kantor. He walked down the aisle, glancing into the stalls to find a horse. There were four horses in the barn. Each one was large, powerful, and obviously very well cared for.

Curtis chose a big black. He opened the door to the stall and spent a minute calming the animal. The violence that had occurred in the barn had spooked the horse. It didn't take long for Curtis to win her over, and he slipped a bridle over her head and brought her out into the center of the aisle. He chose a saddle and slipped it over the horse's back. He cinched it up and took another glance around the room.

The back door opened suddenly.

'Mack, we got – hey!' a man yelled. He groped for his pistol, but Curtis was already firing. The man took a bullet in the groin and another in the chest before he went down. Boots scuffled behind the barn as Dawson's men responded.

Curtis dragged the horse toward a side door between two of the stalls. He had his hand on the door handle and was just about to open it when a pair of Dawson's men leapt through the back door over the dead body of their friend. They took cover in the first two stalls by the door. The first man was in the stall that contained the body of Mack Kantor.

'Goddamn!' he yelled to the other killer, 'he killed Mack.'

Curtis peered cautiously around the corner of the stall wall toward the center aisle. He was greeted with a bullet, which hit a board a few feet above his head. He pulled his head back and knelt in place, thinking.

'You look like hell, Curtis,' one of the men yelled. 'Mack really did a number on you, didn't he?'

Curtis grinned wryly, despite the pain of his split and swollen lips.

'How's Mack looking, you chickenshit?' he retorted. 'He's a damn sight worse off than I am.'

Curtis could hear footsteps at the back of the building near the door. Another voice entered the conversation.

'All right now,' a man said. 'This ain't going to end well for you, Curtis. Be sensible and surrender. We promise to kill you quick-like.'

The other men laughed.

'That's mighty kind of you,' said Curtis. 'I think I'll stay here, though, if it's all the same to you.'

'Suit yourself. And by the way – if you're figuring on trying to get out that side door there, keep in mind we got a man outside covering it.'

Curtis looked toward the door and swore quietly.

'Y'all think of everything, don't you?' he said acidly.

'That's why Mr Dawson pays us so well.'

More laughs came from the back of the room.

'Take the money while you can,' Curtis advised. 'Dawson's luck is going to run out. When it does, he's going to take all of you down with him.'

'We'll see about that.'

Curtis stiffened when he heard one of the men make a dash down the aisle and dive into one of the stalls not far from Curtis's position. They had him cornered and were going to pin him where he was. He could try to make an escape through the side door, but he knew the man hadn't been lying when he said someone was out there covering it, waiting for Curtis to make a break for it.

There was no way around it; his options were bleak no matter what way you looked at it. His best bet, he thought reluctantly, would be to stand his ground and take out as many of Dawson's men with him as he could. He felt no self-pity or regret, only a fierce determination to make these men pay for what they had done, and what they were about to do.

He'd had no illusions about what the consequences might be for allowing himself to be entangled in the conflict between Clem Dawson and the ranchers of Junction City. He'd had high hopes for a positive outcome, but that appeared impossible now – at least for him. But if he could take two or three of the men in the barn with him, then he would give the Bannermans and their neighbors that much more of a fighting chance.

The man who'd moved a few stalls closer to Curtis made a break for the stall beside him. Curtis was ready.

He leapt to his feet and raised his pistol. This time he didn't show himself in the center aisle, but stood up over the plank wall of the stall just as the man dived into the straw that was strewn across the hardpacked dirt floor. Curtis recognized Ike Gibson, who screamed in terror when he spied Curtis looking down at him. A blast from Mack Kantor's pistol silenced the scream instantly. Curtis returned to a crouching position behind the wall.

'So much for your friend,' he taunted.

Enraged, the gunmen responded with brute force. They sprayed the wall and floor around him with one bullet after another. One stray slug found its way into the horse's head. The animal made a strangled noise and fell onto the floor near Curtis, nearly crushing one of his legs as it collapsed. Fragments of wood burst around him and fell into his hair and onto his shoulders.

Finally the fusillade ended. Curtis could hear the men reloading their pistols.

'We're coming for you, you son of a bitch!' someone yelled.

Curtis opened the cylinder on his pistol and inserted another bullet. He wanted to be fully loaded when he made his last stand.

Then he heard the thunder of approaching horse hoofs and the eruption of gunfire outside. The horses drew closer and a man screamed in the yard.

Abe Bannerman's voice sounded and Curtis knew that the tables had turned.

CHAPTER ELEVEN

Curtis heard the horses pull up in the yard, followed by the sounds of the riders dismounting.

'Will!' yelled Abe Bannerman. 'Will – you around?'

'I'm in here,' Curtis called back.

'Can you come out?'

Curtis looked toward the door. The dead horse's body had fallen in such a way as to block the door from opening. It had to weigh over a thousand pounds and Curtis knew he couldn't move it.

'No. I'm stuck in here. Along with three of Dawson's boys.' He called to the gunmen crouching in the barn. 'You hear that, gentlemen? You're through. There ain't no getting out of here alive if you fight.'

'Same goes for you, Curtis,' one of the men responded defiantly.

Despite the bravado, Curtis could tell that much of the fight had gone out of whoever it was who'd uttered those words. Dawson's men were beaten and they knew it. The only question now was whether they'd listen to reason and surrender or decide to go out in a futile blaze of glory.

The answer came sooner than Curtis expected.

Shots were fired near the rear of the barn, and Curtis realized that Dawson's men were exchanging fire with Bannerman and the other homesteaders, who were now clustered at the back of the building.

He rose and looked over the top of the stall wall. He could only see one of the men, three stalls down on the opposite side of the aisle. The man was distracted, firing toward the back door. Curtis lifted his gun and shot him dead where he sat, his bullet entering the left side of the man's head. Now only two of Dawson's killers remained in the barn. When they saw their partner dead in the stall, they decided that discretion was truly the better part of valor.

'All right,' the man closest to the back door hollered when there was finally a break in the gunfire, 'we're ready to give up. No more shooting.'

'Throw your pistols into the aisle,' Bannerman said.

Curtis heard the guns clatter into the dirt.

'Get your hands in the air and step out of the stalls. Two of your pards died out at Phil Shirreffs's place this morning because they decided to make a last stand. Don't be stupid like them.'

Seconds later the men emerged from the stalls, their hands raised obediently. Bannerman had them turn around to prove that they didn't have other weapons on them. Once that had been confirmed, he came into the barn, a pistol in each hand. He was followed by Mike Tancred and Gil Harmon.

'Will,' he called, as Tancred and Harmon tied up the gunmen.

Curtis stepped out from the small passageway from which he and the horse had almost escaped. Bannerman was clearly shocked by his friend's appearance.

'Judas, Will! What happened?'

Curtis walked toward Bannerman and pointed at the body of Mack Kantor.

'I ran into an old friend,' he said. 'He had a little fun at my expense.'

'My God, I guess so,' Bannerman said. He looked at Kantor's body. The knife wound gaped in the dead man's neck. 'Glad to see you returned the favor.'

'It was the least I could do.'

Bannerman put his hand on Curtis's shoulder.

'Damn, Will. I'm glad to see you're in one piece, even if you're not looking so good.'

Curtis chuckled despite himself.

'Thanks, Abe,' he said. 'I think.'

'You know about Jake Douglas and John Wilson?'

'Yes. I saw it happen. You know Dawson hired Cobb McGillicutty to run y'all off your land?'

'I heard. Pretty hard to believe.'

'Believe it.'

They followed Tancred and Harmon out into the yard as they led Dawson's men, who were now bound. Four other of Bannerman's neighbors were sitting their mounts in the yard.

'Glad to see you brought reinforcements, Abe. How's Sally holding up?'

'She's doing fine. I made her head home rather than come into town. She wasn't too happy about that. She took out one of Dawson's bushwhackers out at Phil Shirreffs'.'

'What?'

'She's a hell of a shot, Will.'

'So you've told me.'

Curtis paused by a trough at the back of the barn. He stripped his shirt off and dunked his head into the frigid water, gasping as he pulled it back out. He repeated the process, and soaked his shirt in the water, getting some of the blood and most of the vomit off it. Then he put it back on and buttoned it up.

'Let's head over to Dawson's place and finish this thing,' he said.

The homesteaders split up, with half the group approaching Dawson's house from the alley and the other half approaching along Main Street. Tancred stayed at the barn with the two prisoners.

Alerted by the gunfire at the barn, several of the residents of Junction City watched the horsemen from their porches.

'God bless you!' one elderly woman called from the open second-floor window of her home. Abe Bannerman nodded at her, his jaw set with determination.

The men in the alley dismounted and left their horses tied to a fence a few doors down from Dawson's house. They approached the house with guns drawn, which was just as well, for they were greeted with gunfire from the back porch and the trees near the fence.

Curtis and Bannerman dismounted and tied their mounts to a hitching post at the bank. Curtis read the sign at the front of the building: Bank of Junction City, Est. 1876, Clement F. Dawson, President.

Not for much longer, he thought.

They had reached the edge of the fence in front of the house when they heard the gunshots in the back. Both men had already drawn their pistols.

'Cover me, Abe,' Curtis said.

He leapt over the fence into the yard and knelt behind some rose bushes. His eyes scanned the windows and the porch for any signs of movement. He saw nothing.

Still in a crouching position, he moved rapidly across the yard to the edge of the porch. He expected someone to take a shot at him anytime, but nothing happened. Cautious, he waited a little longer, looking toward Abe Bannerman to make sure the man was still covering him. He was.

Curtis relied on speed to get him safely to the front door. He flattened himself against the wall beside the door and then dared to take a peek through the ornate decorated glass into the entryway. There was no sign of movement there. He reached down and tried the knob.

To his surprise it was unlocked. He looked one last time through the window in the door before he pushed it open and stepped into the house, his pistol extended in front of him.

Guns continued to explode behind the house, helping to muffle the sounds of movement inside. Curtis took a few steps and moved toward the wide-arched entrance to the living room. Right as he looked into the room, a large man pivoted from his position near the fireplace and fired at him. Curtis dived forward and hit the floor in the hallway, on the other side of the archway. The bullet smacked into the wall not far from where Curtis had been standing a moment before.

Curtis rolled over onto his back, his gun raised, and the gunman jumped through the hallway in pursuit of his quarry. Their eyes met and Curtis recognized the face of Cobb McGillicutty.

'Curtis!' yelled McGillicutty.

The killer was so shocked to find Curtis alive that he momentarily gave his opponent an advantage. Curtis brought up his left hand and fanned the hammer on his pistol, sending four shots into McGillicutty's torso before the latter could get another word out. McGillicutty gasped, his face distorted, and fell backward through the open front doorway onto the porch.

Curtis sat up and looked toward the killer. The acrid gunsmoke dissipated and he saw that McGillicutty was no longer a threat to anyone.

He also realized that the shooting behind the house

had stopped. His mind was just registering the change when he heard rapid footfalls up on the second floor. He lunged to his feet and made his way to the staircase.

A feeling of déjà vu came over him as he ascended the steps, his pistol at the ready. He recalled a night just a couple months ago when he'd climbed these stairs in pursuit of Clem Dawson, and now here he was again. That time, both men had survived their encounter. This time, however, only one man would emerge alive. Curtis knew there was no other way.

No one stood at the top of the landing and Curtis covered the last five steps in two quick leaps. The hallway was empty, but the door to Clem Dawson's bedroom was wide open.

'Dawson?' Curtis called, his voice reverberating off the walls. 'You're finished. Come out and face the music.'

There was no response.

Curtis moved forward down the hallway toward Dawson's bedroom. He halted a few feet from the open doorway. He could see part of the room from where he stood. On a desk on the far side of the bedroom was an open leather valise, beside which stood two tall stacks of paper money. Clem Dawson was doing some packing.

Impulsively, Curtis jumped through the doorway into Dawson's room. He swung the gun from left to right, covering the entire room. Dawson was nowhere to be seen. Curtis parted the curtains and looked down into the back yard. He saw Gil Harmon's body in the alley, and the bodies of two of Dawson's men in the grass. Dean Taggart and three other homesteaders were moving out of their covered positions and moving toward the back of the house.

Hinges creaked behind him and Curtis twirled, thumbing back the hammer on his gun. In the doorway of his son's bedroom across the hall stood Clem Dawson, a shotgun gripped in his hands. His clothes were disheveled and his face glistened with sweat. His bloodshot eyes regarded Curtis with unalloyed hatred.

Curtis's hand was perfectly steady as he stared back at Dawson. The air between them seemed charged with danger.

'You're done,' Curtis said. 'Put the gun down or you'll be carried out of this house boots first.'

'You don't know what you've done, Curtis,' said Dawson, his voice trembling with barely controlled frenzy. 'You should never have gotten involved in my affairs.'

'Tell that to Tabor Evans.'

Dawson glared at Curtis and a drop of sweat fell from one of his pasty jowls. Then he bared his teeth and Curtis saw his finger tighten on both triggers of the shotgun.

A gunshot sounded and Dawson's eyes widened with horror and disbelief. His fingers loosened of their own accord and the shotgun fell onto the expensive rug on which Dawson stood. Dawson clutched the bullet wound in his side and turned to his right.

'You!' he shrieked to someone out of Curtis's line of sight.

Another shot came from the place where Dawson was looking. Then another. The banker struggled to say something else, but nothing came from his mouth other than an anguished croak. He fell backwards onto a velvet sofa behind him before falling forward onto the floor. He didn't move again.

Curtis looked down at his gun, his mind not quite comprehending how Dawson had died.

'C'mon in, Curtis,' called a voice from the room across the hall. 'I'm all done shooting now.'

A pistol was tossed onto the rug in the room across the hall from Curtis, who stepped forward and looked in. Alvin Dawson sat in his expensive wheelchair, his legs covered by a blanket. The look he gave Curtis contained no rancor, and the latter realized that the younger Dawson wasn't a threat to him.

'I'm done,' Alvin Dawson said plainly, his eyes resting on the body of his dead father. 'I'm all done.'

Curtis took in the scene for a moment before he went down the stairs and called to Abe Bannerman to let him know it was safe to come in now.

CHAPTER TWELVE

Within a few weeks life had largely returned to normal in Junction City. The revelation of Clem Dawson's murderous activities made the front pages of almost every newspaper in Oregon, and the front pages of several out-of-state papers as well. The governor, stung by the accusation that he might have been inappropriately involved with the elder Dawson, had a new district attorney appointed in Eugene. Only one of Dawson's gunmen survived the shoot-out in the banker's yard, and he was convicted of a variety of crimes and sent up to the state penitentiary in Salem.

The new prosecutor declined to bring charges against Alvin Dawson for the shooting of Clem Dawson. Given the young man's physical and mental condition, it was doubtful he would have survived a trial to begin with. Also, his father's reputation was now so black that much of the public approved of the son's actions. He inherited his father's fortune but remained in isolation in the Dawson home. He had no visitors apart from his servants.

The former vice-president of the Junction City bank took over its operations. The sign with Clem Dawson's name on it was removed from the front of the establishment.

On a cold morning almost exactly a month after the shoot-out at Dawson's, Will Curtis sat on Abe Bannerman's porch, smoking a cigarette and chatting with Maggie Bannerman. He had mostly recovered from his last encounter with Mack Kantor, who was buried in an unmarked grave in the Junction City cemetery along with each of Dawson's other dead gunmen.

'Well, Will – what are your plans now?' asked Maggie, trying to keep her tone casual as she sat knitting in the porch's rocking-chair.

'I don't rightly know,' Curtis said.

He knew why Maggie was asking the question. He'd been back on his feet for more than a week now, and there was nothing keeping him in Junction City: no family, no house, no business. A private person, he hadn't felt comfortable broaching the subject of his plans.

'You still thinking about going down to your sister's place?'

'That probably wouldn't be a bad move for me,' he said. 'They say there're a lot of opportunities down there for people who want land of their own.'

Maggie was silent, her brow furrowed. She'd been confident before the shoot-out that Curtis would stay around, and maybe even marry Sally. Perhaps seeing the cold-blooded murders in Phil Shirreffs's yard, along with the torture he'd suffered at the hands of Mack Kantor, had changed Curtis's mind about Junction City.

The rumble of approaching horses ended the conversation. Curtis still felt a little tingle in his stomach when he heard that sound, something that had never been true before his arrival in this small Oregon town. He had to remind himself that Clem Dawson was dead, along with Cobb McGillicutty and the rest of the banker's henchmen. The sound of horses' hoofs was no longer a harbinger of danger in these parts.

Abe Bannerman emerged into the yard, followed closely by his sister. Maggie rose and put down her knitting.

'I'm going to put on some coffee,' she said.

Curtis stepped down into the yard as she went into the cabin.

'Morning, Sally,' he said with a smile.

The two riders drew reins and dismounted.

'Good morning, Will,' said Sally Bannerman.

'Abe, I'll be ready to help you chop wood any time you're ready,' Curtis said. 'First, I'd like to talk to Sally for a few minutes.'

Abe Bannerman glanced between his sister and the cowboy, then nodded and headed for the front door of the house.

Sally gave Curtis a curious look, with just a hint of anxiety in her face. She, too, had noticed the brooding indecision in him over the last month.

'What did you want to talk about, Will?' she asked.

'Well ...' he began. There was uncertainty in his voice. 'Are you still thinking about rebuilding your pa's saloon?'

Sally thought that was an improvised question rather than what Curtis really wanted to discuss.

'Yes,' she replied. 'I'm thinking about it.' She waited a moment. 'Why do you ask?'

Curtis shrugged nonchalantly.

'That'll probably keep you real busy,' he said.

'It's a demanding job, running a saloon.'

'I'm sure it is.' He raised his eyes and met her gaze. 'Dangerous, too.'

She smiled.

'Sometimes, yes.'

'Kind of job where a woman might want to have a man around,' he opined, grinning. 'You never know who might come into a saloon and cause problems.'

'That's true,' she said, her heart pounding.

'That's why I've been thinking that, um – maybe it would be a good idea for me stay around Junction City. Just in case you need some help.'

Curtis reached out and took Sally's hand, drawing her close to him. He kissed her gently, then held his hands on her shoulders as they looked into each other's eyes.

'You just want to stay around in case I need help?' she asked, with mock coyness.